The Back Road
TO SUCCESS

ALL ROADS ARE NOT PAVED

I0548456

Robert L. Weaver

DiamondStar Reading, LLC.

ISBN: 978-0-9962877-0-8

PRINTED IN THE UNITED STATES OF AMERICA

Dedication

I dedicate this book to all my family members, my close friends, and everyone that encouraged me to continue to strive to make this work. I also want to say that without the help of God, I would not have had the patience, the motivation, nor the knowledge to complete such a challenging task as writing a book!

Contents

Introduction

The following pages contain the story of a young man that found his way in the world by trial and error. It could be the story of your son or daughter or the story of yourself. After all, anyone could have followed these footsteps. So, if this story seems true or you think you might know this person, it's only a coincidence.

The young man's name is Star Wainwright. A very unusual name for a kid growing up in a small southern town. His name was actually given to him by his uncle. It just so happened that on the same night Star was born, the sky was filled with an unusual number of stars. Back in those days, babies were not always born at the hospital. They were born in their parents' houses with a midwife at the mother's bedside. The midwife served as the delivering doctor. Star's uncle was outside the house awaiting the arrival of his new nephew or niece and noticed the large number of stars filling the sky on that warm summer night in June. At first, Star's mother was hesitant to give her new son that name when it was first suggested to her by her brother. But the longer she looked down on her new baby, the more she could see him as her little Star.

His goal was to join the military right after high school graduation. He was one of those kids that thought college was not for him. Like many kids his age, he did not take the college prep classes in high school nor did he take advantage of other opportunities that presented themselves to him so that he could prepare himself for college. Star would say to his friends and anyone else who would listen, "I'm going to join the military right out of high school and let Uncle Sam guide me on a journey around the world!" The idea of going to college was far removed from Star's mind since he had his mind set on joining the military, but unfortunately, Star never made any plans to join the military either. It turned out that his immediate plan was to relax around his house for the first couple of weeks after graduation. Sometimes, the best thought out plans have a way of being changed due to unforeseen circumstances or merely a change of mind.

For Star, it was his plans of relaxing around the house that changed. He had really wanted to join the military. In fact, several years earlier, he had sent a letter requesting to see if he could join the Marines. He wanted to become one of *The Few, The Proud, The Marines!* He waited for weeks for the reply from the Marines recruiter. When he finally received the reply from the recruiter, it was a rejection letter and a few Marine stickers. Typed on the letter in one sentence was "APPLY WHEN YOU ARE OLDER, SON." Star couldn't imagine why a recruiter would send him such a letter! He had spoken with older men who said they had joined the military at an early age so why was he being rejected now? Thinking of the rejection letter reminded him of the time when he tried out for the football team. He was only 5'9" tall and weighed around 130lbs. On the first day of tryouts, the coach came over to Star and told him, "Son, come back and try out when you are bigger!"

Star grew up in a family that had very little money. His mother was unable to work due to health issues, so his family had to make ends meet from what little the government provided on a monthly basis, and from what his older brother and sister provided.

He had many mixed-up dreams about becoming this or that but he never really focused on any one field. The one thing that Star refused to talk about with anyone was going to college. He said, "College is too expensive. The classes are too hard. And I don't have the time to devote any thought to something I don't have an interest in doing."

Chapter 1
High School

My name is Star Wainwright. I attended Asbury High School, home of the Fighting Rams. At the time, the school had only about 700 students attending. That number included students from the 8th grade class. The older kids called the eighth graders "little sheep" as they welcomed them to the high school. Of course, the eighth graders didn't know they were being labeled little babies by being called little sheep. Every incoming eighth grade class had some type of name that signified they were new to high school. The teachers didn't like the way the eighth grade class was "welcomed" to high school so they threatened to send anyone who called the eighth graders little sheep to the principal's office.

The school itself was quite large compared to other schools in the area. The school was located about two miles south of town. I'm not sure why the school wasn't in the city part of town… maybe it was because of the large number of students that lived outside the city limits. The school didn't have a second floor or basement and the largest building at the school was the gymnasium. The football field was also located next to the school. Although there were usually large crowds at the football games, the opposing team often left town with the victory.

Most kids rode the school bus to Asbury High and, of course, I was one of those kids. Once I tried playing hooky with Spencer, my best friend in high school. Spencer's grandmother stayed two houses away from my house and Spencer had spent the night with his grandmother so he had to ride the same bus that I rode to get to school that day. My mother didn't drive nor did Spencer's grandmother. So we purposely missed the bus by taking our time walking up the hill to the main highway where the bus stop was located. Our plan was sound, except neither of us factored in getting told to walk to school by my mother and his grandmother and to have the principal call them once we arrive at the school. That was the first and last time I ever thought about missing a free ride to school!

My house was located within the city limits of town but it really seemed more like I lived in the deep woods. After turning off the main road that led into and out of town, there was a winding dirt road that led down a hill past Spencer's grandmother house to my house. There were a couple other houses on both sides of that road and trees as far as the eye could see behind those houses. It was at the top of this hill at the main highway where all the neighbor kids that stayed on that street caught the bus to Asbury High School.

One day, near the end of my twelfth grade year, I was sitting at the lunchroom table with a few other classmates. I normally sat with Spencer Woods, my best friend in high school. I had known Spencer since the fourth grade. I didn't have a lot of close friends in high school but Spencer was my closest and best friend. Today was one of those days that Spencer had been called home early by his parents. Spencer was saying something about his dad needing help around his farm as he raced down the hall to the main entrance of the school. I gathered from the excitement in his voice that his dad was waiting outside for him at the main entrance of the school. Sitting at the lunchroom table with me was Roy Jones, Stephanie Louis, Mary Taylor, Buddy Drew, and Albert Stein. We were all in the senior class except for Stephanie. Stephanie was a junior but she was the assistant to the senior class president, Mary Taylor. As senior class president, Mary was allowed to choose a junior as her assistant and she choose Stephanie.

"Star, where is your sidekick, Spencer? You guys always sit

together at lunch. I bet he's gotten into some kind of trouble and he's sitting in the principal's office!" It was Albert Stein talking. Known as the class know-it-all, he thought he knew everything about everyone. The really bad part about him thinking he knew everything was when he didn't know something about someone, he made it up!

"No, he has some type of job that he has to do with his dad on their farm," I said. "And why do you always think Spencer is in trouble?"

"Because he's always in trouble and I'm surprised you are not sitting in the principal's office next to him. I don't remember a time when one of you were in the principal's office without the other. It has always been both of you in trouble at the same time!" Albert said.

I didn't have a reply to that comment because it was mostly true. Spencer and I had only gotten in trouble twice that I could remember and both times we were sitting in the principal's office at the same time!

"What? No smart remark, Falling Star?!" It was Albert still talking.

Anytime there were females around, Albert tried to show off and his cousin Buddy sitting next to him didn't help the situation. So I tried to put my attention back on my plate with the half-eaten hamburger and fries that I was happily having before I was interrupted.

Stephanie and Mary had been talking quietly together and never really looked in my direction.

"Hey, Star. Don't let Albert talk to you like that." It was Buddy Drew talking now. Albert's local muscle man and cousin. I knew it wouldn't be long before Buddy would put his two cents into the conversation.

"What are you going to do after high school?" It was the soft voice of Stephanie Louis. I knew right away she was trying to change the subject. Good thing too because it was just about to get ugly for someone!

Stephanie was talking to Buddy and she continued, "I heard you got a scholarship to play football at the University of Alabama."

"Yes I did," said Buddy with a big grin on his face. "I can hardly wait until I start college. I went on a visit to the campus last month and let me tell you, that campus seems to be as big as our entire town!" He was waving his arms in a circular motion to demonstrate the size of the University of Alabama campus.

Roy and Albert both said they were joining the Navy after high school and, of course, everyone knew about the four-year scholarship that Mary Taylor had to attend Georgia Tech.

I really wanted to ask Buddy how he managed to get a scholarship to play football at the University of Alabama. I knew he was some kind of freak athlete, but I only had a couple of classes with him. He didn't impress me at all in any of the classes we had together. But this probably wasn't the best time to be asking him that. I would have to ask Buddy another time about how he managed to get into college.

"What are you planning on doing when you get out of school, Star?" It was Mary Taylor speaking. She was one of the smartest kids in the senior class. She was sitting across from me at the lunchroom table munching on an apple. I'm sure I had a puzzled look on my face. One, because I was surprised that she was actually speaking to me, and two, because she wanted to know my plans after high school. Although she was class president, she had a small group of friends that consisted mostly of the "smarter" kids in school.

"I'm planning on join the military. I'm going to let Uncle Sam pay my way around the world!" I said in grand fashion.

"Sounds exciting but you will never join the military, Star," she said.

I couldn't believe what I just heard! Could this be pick-on-Star day or something? It was bad enough that I had to listen to loud-mouth Albert and his muscle-bound cousin, Buddy. Now I had to take shots from Ms. Smarty Pants Taylor!

"How do you know what I'm going to do?" I responded with a little agitation in my voice. Mary Taylor had said little to nothing to me the past four years. How could she possibly know what I was going to do after high school?

"Have you looked in the mirror lately?" she went on. "You were too scrawny to play football and I probably could out-jump you."

Just because I had tried out for the football team and was cut on the first day of tryouts didn't mean I couldn't join the military! Now I was really beginning to get upset! Both Buddy and Albert looked on with huge smiles on their faces and both were beginning to laugh but neither stepped in with a comment. Even Stephanie seemed to be laughing. Albert and his cousin were really enjoying how Mary was talking to me. It appeared that we had an audience since a few of the other students sitting at the surrounding tables began to turn their attention to our table.

Now it was a matter of pride for me. It was one thing to have rough and tough guys speak that way to me but it was a completely different story when it came down to a girl speaking that way to me. Especially when it was in front of a crowd of students!

"Why are you saying that?" I asked in a deeper voice trying to sound bigger than I felt.

"Look," Mary said. "I wouldn't be having this conversation with you if it wasn't for a class project that I'm doing in Mr. Thomas' college prep class.

I knew Mr. Thomas. He was one of the coolest teachers at Asbury High. I was in his twelfth grade history class and that class was one of the two classes that I actually enjoyed attending. It didn't matter what topic we were having that day, Mr. Thomas knew how to make a history class fun.

"What are you talking about?" I asked Mary.

She said, "Mr. Thomas assigned me to you. I asked him to assign me to a different classmate but all he said was that you would benefit the most from this project. I'm telling you right now I don't see you ever joining the military and neither do I see you ever going to any college. You probably haven't made any plans to join the military because if you had, you would already know where you were headed by now. Roy and Albert know exactly when and where they are to report after graduation. As for college, you wouldn't know a college application if it landed on your nose!"

That drew laughter from everyone at our table and I could hear kids at nearby tables laughing.

"Wait! What?" I said, trying hard to raise my voice just loud enough to be heard over the laughter.

"Who said anything about me going to college? I have no intentions of going back to school after having just left school after twelve years. So whatever Mr. Thomas or anyone else for that matter have planned for me can forget it! As far as me joining the military, I don't have to join immediately out of school. I can wait as long as I want before I join," I said in my best telling-her-off voice.

All Mary said to that was, "Exactly!"

She then picked up her tray with the half-eaten chicken pot-pie, walked over to the trash container to dispose of what was not eaten, and left the lunchroom.

Stephanie looked at me and then at the other students sitting at the table and said, "Bye, guys." She then quickly put her food tray away and followed Mary out the lunch room.

Some of the other kids sitting near our table had turned around to see what the loud talking was about but after Mary stormed out, most of them went back to the business of having lunch. I overheard one of the kids sitting at the table behind me say, "It was only Star. He was just about to get his butt kicked by a girl, again!" Some kid responded to that saying, "I know, and Spencer isn't with him today."

I don't know what those kids were talking about but I was never beaten by any girl. I called it a draw! Two evenly matched opponents!

"Hey, Falling Star." It was Albert talking. I had completely forgotten about him and his cousin, who were still sitting at the table. "I know you are trying to ignore me but it's not going to work. Everyone knows Mary is right about you. You talk a lot about what you are planning on doing but we all know you are just going to stay at home and let your Mama take care of you!"

That comment drew loud laughter from what seemed like the entire lunchroom! Now I knew it was time for me to end my lunch. I cleaned up what was left from my hamburger and fries and left the lunch room as quickly as I could. I could still hear Albert mouthing off but I completely ignored him and any other comments from the kids I passed on my way out the lunchroom door. It seemed like I couldn't get to my next class fast enough! Strange as it may seem, my next class was Mr. Thomas's history class!

———•《•》•———

As school was letting out later that day, many of the students were headed for their assigned school bus to take them home. The buses were parked at the front entrance of Asbury High in a long line of yellow and black vehicles. Mary Taylor and Stephanie Louis were headed towards the student parking lot. Mary was one of the few students that had a car she could drive to school and today she was giving Stephanie a ride home.

Mary had a red, two-door Ford Mustang. It was equipped with red and black leather interior, bucket seats and a convertible top. Although it was a hot day late in May, she didn't have the roof down. She told other kids that she never liked to ride with the roof down when she had passengers because the noise of the engine and the rush of the wind made it difficult to communicate driving down the highway. Her parents only allowed her to drive the car to school three days a week and maybe to an occasional football or basketball game being held at the high school.

"Why were you so hard on Star, Mary?" Stephanie asked.

"You of all people should already know why, Stephanie," Mary replied. "Don't you remember me telling you about the college prep class that I'm taking?"

"Yes, but I wasn't aware that class had something to do with Star. I know he's never been one of your favorite classmates but usually you never say anything to him," Stephanie said.

"It's because of that project Mr. Thomas has us doing. Our class has seven students in it and Mr. Thomas came up with the idea that each of us should mentor a fellow classmate. We are to discuss life after high school with that student, and talk about what plans they might have after they graduate. We can even make suggestions on what they should do if we want to," Mary said.

"It sure didn't seem like you did any of that with Star today," Stephanie replied.

"Mr. Thomas assigned me to the worst classmate ever! He never tries to do anything and when he does, he falls flat on his face. How can I have a discussion with him about what he's going to do after high school when he is constantly making up stories about joining the military? You heard him today. He hasn't made any plans to do anything after high school. I just don't see what Mr. Thomas sees in him," Mary said.

As they drove past the main entrance of the high school, they could see the students boarding their assigned bus for the trip home.

Stephanie said, "I don't ever recall hearing of a project like the one Mr. Thomas has you guys working on."

"Mr. Thomas' idea is to get three or four kids to try the College Development Program at State University. The program is strictly for graduating seniors that haven't applied for college or been accepted at a college or university. He said that students will stay on campus and attend college classes just as if they were enrolled in college. He assigned all the students in his college prep class one of the seniors from the senior class that hadn't decided to go to college. The students that are assigned to us don't know about this project until we explain it to them. You saw how Star reacted when I mentioned the word college. He has no desire to sit in a college classroom, so how am I going to explain the College Development Program to him when he flat out refuses to listen?" Mary said.

"You were still kind of hard on him," Stephanie replied. "So he's probably never going to listen to you now."

"I know," Mary responded. "But I'm not planning on being soft or easy on him. It's his future that's at stake, not mine!"

They had driven the two miles back to town and were now stopped at the only traffic light in town.

"Besides." Mary said. "We only have a couple more weeks in school before we graduate. I really don't have to bring this subject up again with Star. I'm going to tell Mr. Thomas I spoke with Star and

Star refused to listen to anything I had to say. In fact, I will say Star raised his voice at me and said, 'Anybody that has intentions of me going to college can forget it!'"

———————⟨⟨◉⟩⟩———————

On a warm, sunny afternoon about a week before graduation, Star's sister, Kelly, was giving him a ride to the park since the park was located across town. Most days when Star wanted to play basketball he would either ride his ten-speed bicycle or his older brother would drop him off. Today, Kelly agreed to give him a ride to Mid-Town Park. As the car pulled from the driveway, Kelly said, "Star, next week you will be a high school graduate. Have you considered what you want to do after you graduate? I know there are lots of things you could do but have you given it any thought?"

From time to time, Kelly would ask Star what he wanted to do after high school. Star would generally reply with, "I'm looking into some things." And Kelly would end the conversation about life after high school. This time, Kelly persisted with the question. "What do you mean by you are looking into some things?"

"Why are you asking me that question again, Kelly? I plan on joining the military after high school," Star replied.

"Okay, I know that's what you said you were going to do, so why did you not talk to the recruiters down at the high school?" Kelly asked.

"What? Have you been down to the school nosing around? You of all people need to stay out of my business!" Star exclaimed.

"I wouldn't be in your business if Mother hadn't asked me to go down to the school and talk to the guidance counselor about you. I could have been doing lots of other things. If it wasn't for Mother asking me to go down there, you better bet I wouldn't have been at the school! You've been telling everyone around town how you are going to join the military and let Uncle Sam pay your way around the world but you haven't said anything to Mother about what you are planning on doing after high school. Some of her friends have been asking her what she thinks about you joining the military. How do you think she's been responding to those questions?" Kelly asked.

Star never answered that question because Kelly had just driven into the parking lot of Mid-Town Park. He quickly gathered his basketball and water bottles and said, "Thanks for the ride, Sis. I will see you in a couple of hours."

As he ran off to the basketball court, Kelly, sitting in the car, wondered if he had heard anything she had just said.

His future wasn't one of Star's favorite subjects. He managed to avoid that subject with everyone, including his family and his best friend, Spencer. All he really wanted to do was think about today and let tomorrow take care of itself. Playing basketball was a way for him to take his mind off tomorrow.

Mid-Town Park was small. There was a sand and gravel lot that served as the parking lot for about 15 or 20 vehicles, and there were also a couple of places for small kids to play. Monkey bars, a merry-go-round, and a sand pit made up the kids area. The basketball court was off to the side and several feet away from the small kids play area. The court had a swinging fence door for an entrance and a metal bench on one side of the playing area for players to sit when they were not playing in the game. Mid-Town Park didn't have the one thing that most kids and adults wanted at a park: a working water fountain.

"Look who's here, it's Falling Star!" It was Star's classmates Loud Mouth Albert and of course his cousin, Buddy.

"You come to get schooled in basketball again? I hope you

bought your game today because every other time I've seen you here, you never had it with you!" The comment from Albert drew loud laughter from the majority of the guys sitting at the bench area.

"I've been practicing a lot the past few weeks," Star said. "I know in the past you've been able to get the best of me but that was in the past! Today is a new day!"

"Yeah, right!" responded Albert loudly as usual. "You can't out jump little Mary Taylor, you're slow as molasses, and you can't dribble a basketball, much less shoot one!"

Albert was right in most of his description of me but I had been practicing a lot the past few weeks. I would come here to the park when no one else was around and practice all three of the skills that Albert said I lacked.

The winning team was headed back onto the court and now it was Jay Mills turn to pick the opposing team. Anyone that called 'next game' could pick the team to play against the winning team but only if that person called 'next game' before anyone else called it. The person that had next game could choose anyone to play on their five-man team except those players from the winning team. Generally, the captain that was making the picks chose the taller and bigger players first (normally a couple of players from the losing team) and then the best skilled players would be chosen no matter the size of the player. This method of picking a team was never fair because it normally left several players sitting on the bench game after game waiting to play. So, the best way for those players that never got picked to play on a team was to call next game and be the captain of their own team.

Jay Mills was almost six feet tall but he was a very good basketball player and when he picked his team, he excluded several guys sitting on the bench including me. I had already called to be the next captain after Jay's game because I had a feeling that he wouldn't choose me to be on his team. I also asked Jay why he didn't pick any of the guys that haven't played on any team.

"Because I would like to win at least one game today," he answered.

"You don't think you could win with one or two of the guys that haven't played yet?" I asked.

"No, I don't," he responded as he walked onto the basketball court to start the next game.

As I sat down on the bench waiting for the game to end, Jim Ross sat down next to me.

He was in a couple of my classes in high school. Although he was a regular at the park like most of the guys here today, his basketball skills were similar to mine.

"How's it going, Star?" he asked. Not waiting for me to respond, he continued.

"I can hardly wait until I'm on that plane headed down to South Florida. My older brother sent me a plane ticket to come stay with him for a few weeks. His idea is for me to find a job when I get down there. What about you? What are you planning on doing after graduation?"

That seemed to be the question that everyone was going to ask me whether or not I was willing to answer it.

"Right now, I'm unsure what I'm going to do. Seems like everyone is always asking me what my plans will be after finishing school. Truth is, I haven't made any definite plans," I answered.

"Trying to find a job around this town will be close to impossible unless you want to go work at the Plant. It's just about the only place that will be hiring," Jim said.

The Plant was short for Jack's Poultry Plant. All things chicken all the time is what I called it. It was one of the largest poultry plants in that part of the state. Almost everyone that applied got hired to work there. The Plant has two operating shifts, which consisted of a day shift and a night shift. Fresh chicken was processed at the plant and shipped out from the plant daily.

"Forget that!" I said. "No way am I going to work at Jack's Poultry Plant. I know I would get hired if I applied, but I made a promise to myself that I would never work there. That work is not for everybody and I commend all those folks that work there full-time. Shift work is not for me!"

"That's one of the reason I'm glad my brother sent me a ticket to come to Florida. I'll have a better opportunity to find a different type of job down there," Jim said.

The current basketball game had just ended and now it was my turn to pick a squad to play against the winning team led by Albert. Talking to Jim got me to thinking about what I should be doing after graduation. I had planned on resting and relaxing after graduation so that while I was relaxing I could decide what my next course of action should be. Should I try to get a job or should I just join the military like I've been talking about doing the past few months? At any rate, I should have plenty of time to come up with something while I'm resting!

As the players came off the court, several players from the losing team inquired about who was the next captain and if they could play on the team. I happily informed them I was captain of the next team and the players on my team had already been chosen. My team included three guys standing on the side that hadn't played, Jim and myself.

It turned out to be a quick defeat from the winning team led by Loud Mouth Albert. Albert continued to brag and boast about how he was such a good player and that no team could beat the team he had assembled that day.

After playing a couple of games and losing both times to Albert's team, I decided to call it quits for the day. I'd had enough. All the practicing that I did the prior couple of weeks hadn't paid off. I didn't play any better in the pickup game today than I had played three or four weeks ago. The only positive about today was I felt much better. Unlike in the past, I felt like I still had a lot of energy to run up and down the basketball court.

Chapter 2
Job Search

Graduation had finally come and gone and now I was relaxing at home. A few days ago, I had taken the next step in my life. I had graduated from high school and now I was free to do just about anything I wanted to do. At the moment, I was thinking about how long I should sit around my Mom's house. Many of the kids in my senior class were either getting ready to go off to college or to join the military. A couple of my classmates had actually found work around town and a few others were working on their family farm like Spencer.

Spencer had asked me once to come work on his Dad's farm just to see if I liked farm work. It just so happened that the day I went out to Spencer's Dad's farm was the same day that the bales of hay had to be gathered from the field. It took Spencer and me, along with two farmhands, all day to transport all the hay from the field to the barn where the hay would be stored.

One farmhand drove a tractor with a flatbed wagon attached to it. Although the wagon was flat to begin with, we could add rails to make the sides higher as we loaded the bales of hay. The wagon was able to handle 50 or 60 bales easily if they were stacked correctly. The other farmhand was responsible for stacking the bales and installing the rails as needed. Spencer and I had the task of loading the bales onto the wagon. Each bale of hay weighed anywhere between 75 and 90 pounds. The bales were in 2 or 3-foot square bundles held tightly together with straps of cord. Spencer was positioned on one side of the trailer and I was on the other side. As we walked past a bale on our side, we would toss it onto the trailer so that the farmhand could stack it neatly. At first, it was somewhat easy, but as the temperature began to rise and the number of bales I had to toss onto the trailer begin to grow, I quickly learned that farming probably wasn't for me! I was sore for days after that trial run at becoming a farmhand.

I couldn't believe I was out of high school. No more homework, no more running to catch the bus, and no more teachers! Although a couple of the teachers were really cool, I preferred to keep my distance from them. Teachers like Mr. Thomas were an exception. He made going to school fun. He would come up with some type of history learning game to keep the kids in his class interested. We all enjoyed trying to beat him at the game he came up with. Although he won most of the history games, a couple of times the students left the class victorious. He finally got around to telling me about that college development program during the last week of school. That was what Mary Taylor was trying to talk to me about in the lunchroom a few weeks ago.

He called me into his classroom, which also served as his office. I wasn't too surprised that he called me into his room. I thought it was about a late paper that I had turned in or about how I didn't do so well on the last test he had given to the class. But to my surprise, he had a smile on his face as I sat down in the chair in front of his desk.

"What are your plans after graduation?" he asked right away.

I was caught completely off guard with that question.

"I'm not sure, Mr. Thomas, I thought about joining the military and seeing the world," I responded.

"Have you thought about going to college?" he asked.

"No, not really. I haven't given it any serious thought. But why are you asking me about college?"

"Mary Taylor told me about a conversation she had with you in the lunchroom a few weeks ago, Star. She told me how you said you didn't want to have anything to do with college. After hearing that, I thought it might be in your best interest to sign you up in a summer introductory college prep class. It's a two-week course sponsored by the college to give students a chance to see what college life is all about. You will stay in a college dorm with a roommate that's also taking the course and you will be required to attend class just as if you were going to college," he said.

Forgetting for a moment I was talking to a teacher, I almost started to raise my voice, but I caught myself before I made that blunder!

"Why did you enroll me in that class, Mr. Thomas?" I asked.

"Because I think you have the ability to go to college and succeed," he answered.

I was very much surprised at that comment. Not one teacher during the prior four years of high school had suggested anything to me about going to college! Now, literally at the end of my high school career, I was talking to a teacher about college. Not only was that teacher asking me about college, that same teacher actually thought I might have the ability to succeed in college!

I was almost sure I wanted to do anything but go to college. I never thought about college and when I did think about it, the same question kept coming to my mind. How could I compete with all those smart kids? Kids like Mary Taylor had a special talent for learning. It almost seemed like she could just look at a book and know all the material inside it! I didn't have the talent for learning. School for me was like the time I practiced basketball for weeks. No matter how much I practiced, I was no better at the sport than when I first started practicing! I didn't have a choice but to tell Mr. Thomas that I wasn't interested in college.

"I don't know Mr. Thomas. I had high hopes of joining the military. I plan on going to the recruiting station in a couple of months to apply," I said.

"So does that mean you haven't signed any formal papers obligating you to the military?"

"No, I was planning on relaxing for a couple of months. The last four years of high school have been difficult," I said.

"Since you haven't signed paperwork to join the military, you could at least think about the program. You don't have to make a decision until the end of the month," he said.

"Star! Are you listening to me?"

It was my Mom! She was standing inside the doorway to my room. I had been so deep in thought about the conversation with Mr. Thomas I hadn't noticed my mother standing in the doorway to my room.

"Yes, Mother. I'm listening," I said quickly. I wanted to distract her from the fact that I was daydreaming and not listening to her.

"It's time for you to go out and look for a job. I will not have one of my children sitting around the house just being lazy! It's one thing if you don't find a job after looking for one, but it's an entirely different story if you are not trying to find some place to hire you. Jack's Poultry Plant is always looking to hire students that just graduated from high school," she said.

"No way am I going to go work at the Plant!" I said loudly. "Not that I'm too good to work there, I just can't do that type of work!"

"I know you are not raising your voice at me!" my mother said even louder than before.

"No mother, I'm not raising my voice at you. I would never do that. I just don't want to work at Jack's Poultry plant," I said, hoping she would understand.

"Just start your job search as soon as possible," she said.

"Yes, mother, I will start my job search tomorrow," I said more quietly.

I knew finding a job in a small town would be difficult and close to impossible. Mr. Thomas's idea about the college prep program was starting to sound a whole lot better. I think Mr. Thomas had mentioned something about the college paying me money if I attended. I really did want to join the military, but I wasn't ready to do all the physical work involved when joining the military. A four-week college course just to see what college life was all about was beginning to sound better and better with every passing second!

<hr>

Just as I had promised my mother, I was up early the next day headed out to look for employment. My plan was to go visit all the local businesses in town and ask if they needed help, then hopefully they would hire me.

The sun was shining bright and the temperature had already begun to rise. I didn't have a car and my bicycle had a flat tire. That left me with the only other choice I had since neither my brother nor my sister was available to give me a ride. That choice was to walk.

There was nothing unusual about me walking the two miles to town. I had made that trip many times in the past. I just didn't want to walk in the rising heat because I wanted to be as fresh as possible when I spoke to the store managers. The walk to Town Square was a continuous walk uphill. The first part of the walk from my house had me walking up a hill about the distance of two football fields just to get to the main highway that led to town. From the main highway, I would travel west up a sloping hill for about two miles until I reached Town Square.

The main highway was a two-way road that went straight through the heart of town. The 30 mile per hour speed zone and the one traffic light were two of the three things that could cause travelers to stop. The third thing that got travelers to stop more often than the traffic light was the gas stations located at the intersection of the traffic light. There was not another gas station for miles once a traveler had left town.

There was no one else walking on the sidewalk that morning and only a couple of cars passed by me as I made my way towards Town Square. There were houses on both sides of the road and occasionally a face could be seen peering out a window.

The walk took about 30 minutes. I was beginning to feel the heat pressing down on me and I was glad to see the sign pointing towards O'Reilly's grocery store. The grocery store was going to be the first stop on my hunt for a job. If all went well, I would be bagging groceries before the end of the day!

O'Reilly's grocery store was a small building like many of the other establishments in town. The two doors at the front right corner of the building served as the entrance and the exit. There were also three large glass windows off to the right side of the entrance/exit doors. Each window had a large banner hanging from it. Each banner advertised a different weekly special. One banner read '*Pork Chops $.49 a lb. The Price This Month!*' The other two banners advertised coffee and vegetables. Each banner had large red and black writing on a white background.

As I walked inside the store, the cool air from the air conditioner hit me in the face and it felt very refreshing coming in from the mid-morning heat.

"Hello, Star, how's your mother doing?"

It was Mr. Terry. He was leaving the store with a bag of groceries in his arms. He was also one of my Mother's elderly friends. Mr. Terry would do odd jobs around the house and occasionally drop off some fresh fruit and vegetables and give them to her.

"She's doing well, Mr. Terry."

"Tell her I asked about her," he said.

"I will," I responded as he continued out the door.

My mother knew a lot of people in this small town and during my search for employment that morning, a lot of people asked me to give their well wishes to my mother once I returned home.

Mr. O'Reilly had owned that grocery store for more than twenty years. His claim to fame was that he had the freshest vegetables in town. It was hard to argue that, since a lot of what he sold came straight from the surrounding farms.

The store had one checkout lane with a cash register on both sides of the lane. Today, Mrs. Carter was the cashier at the cash register. I had been to that store hundreds of times in the past and I never thought about how many employees were actually employed there until today. I remember seeing guys stocking the can foods on the shelf and I knew there were at least two people working in the fresh meat department located at the back of the store. I could picture myself wearing one of Mr. O'Reilly's green uniforms and stocking the canned foods section. I'm sure I wouldn't have a problem doing that kind of work. Especially since I would be working inside in the cool air conditioning!

"Can I help you find something?" Mrs. Carter asked.

"Yes, where is Mr. O'Reilly? I'm looking for a job and I wanted to speak with him about working here. I'm sure I could be a big help around the store," I said, a big smile on my face.

"Mr. O'Reilly is in his office but he will be out shortly. If you wait around at the front of the store, you can't miss him when he comes out," she said.

"Thank you," I said.

I walked over to what I thought would be aisle one, since no aisle had numbers on them. That aisle just happened to be the fresh vegetable aisle. Standing in this aisle, I could see across the front of the store. The store only had eight aisles so it wasn't difficult to see anyone coming inside the store or leaving to go outside the store.

After a short time, sure enough, Mr. O'Reilly came from the back of the store. He was walking up the vegetable aisle towards the front of the store. Now was my chance to get this job!

"Good morning, Mr. O'Reilly," I said as he approached me. "Can I speak with you about getting a job here?"

"Good morning," he said.

"Aren't you Mrs. Wainwright's youngest son?"

"Yes sir, I am," I responded.

I was sure I was on the inside track to get this job!

"You tell her I said hello when you get back home. As for that job, I'm not looking to bring anyone else onboard right now. The start of summer is generally a slow time for me. I might have something open near the end of August. Right now, I don't have any open positions. If something does come open before then, I will keep you in mind," he said.

"Thank you, Mr. O'Reilly. I will let my mother know you asked about her when I get home," I said.

Wasting no more time in O'Reilly's grocery store, I headed to my next destination to look for a job.

I started my job search with all the confidence in the world that I could find a job. But as that morning slowly turned to early afternoon and the outside temperature rose to the high 90s, my confidence had all but evaporated! Each store or business that I went into gave me a similar story about not needing anyone to work, or that they already had too many employees.

After two weeks, my job search around town had come to a disappointing end. I knew it would be difficult to find a job in a small town but I had no idea that it would be this hard. I probably could get work loading watermelons onto a truck but that job sounded too much like the time I tried loading hay onto a flatbed trailer. Loading hay was just too hard and loading melons sounded very similar.

For two weeks, my Mother had asked me every day how was my job search coming along. She also asked me if I had applied at Jack's Poultry Plant. Every day for the past two weeks I gave her the same answer.

"No, I haven't found a job, and no, I haven't applied for a job at the Plant."

I made a promise to myself never to work at Jack's Poultry Plant. I know my mom probably would love to see me working anywhere at this point. I was going to do all it took to make sure I didn't work at the Plant!

Chapter 3

College Development Program

Growing up in a small town did not offer many opportunities to get a job. In one day, I had gone on a job search and visited all the local businesses in town. It had been just over two weeks since that day, and so far, I hadn't found anything close to a job. I was beginning to run out of options. As long as my Mother didn't come to me and say go to Jack's and apply for a job, I had time. But given her mood towards me the past couple of days, I couldn't count on her not saying that for long. I had to do something or it might come down to me taking a slow ride over to the Plant.

Mr. Thomas's idea of that college development program was beginning to sound like a good idea. What did I have to lose? It was apparent I wasn't finding a job anytime soon on my present course of action. Yes, I talked about wanting to join the military, but I didn't want to do any of that physical work. I talked all that talk about joining the Army but never really had any intention of joining. I hadn't even lasted an hour in the football tryouts. I had trouble with pickup basketball. How could I join something like the army and expect to keep up? A two-week course just to see how college life would be was beginning to sound better and better every second!

After another day of being jobless, I decided to look into that college development program that Mr. Thomas spoke about a few months earlier. He said I was to call down to the high school and speak with the guidance counselor and the counselor would give me all the information I would need.

The next day, I called down to the high school and spoke with Mrs. Wade. I didn't actually know Mrs. Wade but I had seen her a time or two in the hallway and I had heard other kids speak to her. "I was hoping to get a call from you! Mr. Thomas told me you might be calling the school to get the information for the college development program at the State University. The program sounds very exciting and I just know you will love it!"

Mrs. Ward sounded very excited about me calling the school to inquire about the college development program. At first, I wondered why she was so excited, but after thinking about it, I figured she was just doing her job of being a guidance counselor.

"All you have to do is be on campus Sunday the 25th. That's only a few days away so you don't have a lot of time to get ready. You are to meet Mr. Johnson at Assembly Hall at 2 pm. I'm not sure how much you know about the campus but it shouldn't be too difficult to find your way around and locate Assembly Hall. All the instructions you need are in a folder I have for you. Just stop by the high school and I will give it to you. When you get the folder, take some time and go through those papers. All the instructions you need are inside. Do you have any questions?" she asked.

I had a lot of questions but I could only think of one to ask at the moment. "What should I bring with me?"

"Just bring enough clothes for a two-week stay on the campus of State University and an open mind for knowledge," Mrs. Ward said.

"Okay, Mrs. Ward. I will be present and accounted for on Sunday the 25th."

Wasting no time, I picked up the folder from Mrs. Ward that same day. Sunday was only a few days away and after reading those papers, I had several things to do to get ready for a stay on a college campus. The first thing I had to do was inform my Mother of my new plans. I wasn't sure how she would react but I knew she would support whatever decision I made as long as I was making a decision to do something!

Once I returned from picking up the folder from Mrs. Wade, I immediately searched for my mother to inform her about my new plans. I found her sitting in her favorite chair reading a magazine in the living room. She didn't like to be disturbed when she was reading in her favorite chair. She said that was her quiet time.

I walked quietly into the room and said in a quiet voice, "Hello, Mother. I've decided to give college a try. I've signed up for a program at State University that will allow me to give college life a try for a couple of weeks just to see if college is something I might want to pursue."

After a few moments of silence, my mother looked up from the magazine she had been reading. For the first time I could remember, I couldn't read the expression on her face. She didn't seem to be upset. There was something in the way she looked at me that I couldn't read.

"I don't have a problem with you giving college a try as long as it's something you want to do. Neither your brother nor your sister wanted to go to college. But I think that was mainly because I didn't have the money to send them to college. It's going to be the same way with you. I don't have the money to send you to college. If college turns out to be something you want to do, you will have to find a way to pay for it yourself," my mother answered.

My mother didn't say anything else. She had turned her attention back to the magazine she had been reading. That was her way of giving me the okay to try college for a couple of weeks. That also meant that I would have to come up with the money for college if it turned out that was what I wanted to do.

Sunday finally came and I was looking forward to staying on a college campus. But at the same time, I was a little nervous about leaving home. It was only a two-week stay but the longest that I had ever stayed away from home was spending the night at the home of my friend Spencer. I was about seven or eight years old at that time. As I recall, around 10 pm, I had asked Spencer's mom if I could go home. I didn't think that I would be homesick now that I was a little older.

During the past couple of days, I had been collecting and preparing all the necessary items I would need for my stay at State University. The folder that Mrs. Ward gave me contained a list of supplies that I would need. All I had to do was collect those items and bring them with me when I checked into the dormitory. Some of the items on that list were: soap, bath towels, hand towels, gym clothes, extra pair of shoes, extra pair of socks, alarm clock, paper, pens, pencils, and bedding.

But before I could think about staying on campus, I first had to find transportation to the college. I had almost forgotten that I needed to find a way to get to the university. Fortunately, my sister came to my rescue. She agreed to take me to the campus and pick me up when the two weeks were over. All I had to do was wash her car before I left to go, then again when I returned. That was an offer I couldn't refuse.

The drive to State University would take a little more than two hours so I had to be packed and ready to leave home by 11 am. I wasn't too concerned about me being on time, but ensuring my sister wasn't late required a different approach—she wasn't known for her promptness. I enlisted the aid of my mother to help get that accomplished. My mom was one of the best cooks in town. In fact, in her younger years, she was the top cook in the only restaurant in town. On certain Sunday mornings when we were growing up, she would make a large breakfast for my brother, sister, and me. She didn't make those breakfasts as often now because my two siblings had moved out. Since I was going away for a couple of weeks, today was one of those Sundays she made a big breakfast. Bacon, scrambled eggs, cheesy grits, toast, and sausages were on the menu with sliced peaches, apples, and strawberries. So on the Saturday before I was to leave, I reminded Susan not to be late for Sunday morning breakfast. As I expected, that was enough motivation to get her there on time.

My mom enjoyed cooking and would offer to share a meal with anyone. The one thing she didn't like was for her kids to show up for a meal late. Growing up, we would run the risk of waiting until everyone had finished eating or miss out on a delicious dessert! It was no surprise Susan and my older brother showed up on time to enjoy a home cooked breakfast meal.

It was right at 1:30 pm when my sister and I drove up to Assembly Hall. It turned out my sister knew a little about State University. That was news to me since she never indicated to me she had knowledge of the campus. Even during the drive to the college, she didn't say a word about knowing her way around.

There were a couple of students walking across what seemed to be a concrete bridge leading into a building. Other students were sitting underneath a nearby tree on a neatly cut lawn. I had never been to State University but my first impression was a good one. There were a number of students unloading their luggage from cars parked in front of Assembly Hall. Most of those students appeared to be around my age but I wasn't sure of that estimation. They all had something else in common. They had the look of being new to the surroundings and a little uncertain as to what to do. Some were hugging family members and a couple of the female students unpacking seemed to be crying. I guess that's not unusual since they might be leaving loved ones and home for the first time.

Assembly Hall was conveniently located on the front side of campus. Community Avenue was the name of the road that led to the front entrance of the dorm. The building was made up of three connecting large buildings. The small building in which the larger buildings were connected was simply called the Main Lobby. It was one of five dormitories on campus but the only one that was coed. Each connecting building that made up Assembly Hall was four stories high. Each room had a tall window and similar drapes could be seen hanging from all the windows. A couple of the windows had the drapes pulled open to let in the bright sunlight.

The Main Lobby of Assembly Hall was where I was to report. The information in the folder that Mrs. Wade gave me made it clear that I should report to this building because no other dorm was accepting students.

I gathered my suitcase and my gym bag that contained all the supplies I would need from my sister's car. I tucked my pillows beneath my arms, thanked my sister for driving me to campus, and reminded her not to forget to pick me up in two weeks. I said goodbye to her and made my way to the double doors that served as the entrance to Assembly Hall.

The double doors opened directly into the welcome room. A couch, two matching chairs, and a coffee table made up the only furniture in the room. A couple of large, framed pictures of elderly men dressed in caps and gowns were hanging on the wall. Off to the left side of the room was an enclosed reception desk with a young lady at the window talking to two students. The only entrance to the reception desk was a closed door facing the center of the room. As I walked across the room to the couch, a man in his late 30s or early 40s approached me with a huge grin on his face and said, "Are you here for the College Development Program?" Before I could answer, he continued, "I'm James Johnson and I'm the coordinator of the program."

"Yes, I'm here for the program and my name is Star Wainwright," I replied, upbeat and happy. The excitement in my voice made Mr. Johnson even happier.

"Set your luggage over there," Mr. Johnson said, pointing to an area next to the couch. I walked over to the area Mr. Johnson indicated for my luggage and he said, "Lucy will get you checked in and tell you which room you are assigned to and where it's located. Just step up to the window when she finishes checking in the other two students."

When Lucy had finished checking the other two students in, I walked over to the reception station and introduced myself to her.

Lucy proceeded to look through a file beneath the window from which she produced a key on a chain and a pamphlet. "Here you are, Mr. Wainwright. You are assigned to room 5-1 and your roommate's name is Ryan Callahan."

Lucy pointed to a door across the room. "Just walk through that door to get to your room on the first floor. Your roommate has already checked in so he might be in the room. Do you have any questions about the dorm or about the campus in general?"

"I don't have any questions right now," I responded, as if I didn't need to ask any questions about anything.

"If you think of a question about the dorm or about the campus, you probably can find the answers in the pamphlet that I gave you. Oh, meet here in the lobby at 5pm. All the students in the program will meet here and walk over to the Student Center conference room for orientation," Lucy said in a friendly voice.

"Okay, thank you," I responded, walking away to gather my luggage.

The room was very easy to find. After walking through the door Lucy pointed to, I passed a set of stairs that led to the other floors. The rooms were all on the right side of the hallway and they all had numbers on them except for the first door I passed. That door had '*The Room of the RA*' engraved on it. I realized that all the rooms were on the right side of hall for a reason. The reason was because the restrooms and showers were located in the middle section of the hall. Access to the showers could be gained from two sides with the other two sides being closed off. When I reached room 5-1, I unlocked the door and took my suitcase, gym bag, and pillows inside. Lucy was correct in her estimation of Ryan being in the room. When I walked in the room, Ryan, who was sitting at his desk and putting away some of the things he had brought along, looked up and said, "Hey, you must be Star."

I placed my luggage on the only bed that didn't have a bedspread and said, "Yep, I'm Star. And you must be Ryan?"

"Yes, I'm your roommate for the next two weeks. You have a very interesting name. Why did your parents name you Star?" he asked.

"Oh, my name? My uncle gave me that name when I was born. The sky was filled with stars the night I was born so he thought I should be named Star," I said, answering his question about my name and hoping he wasn't one of those guys that liked to asked relentless questions.

"And your mom listened to him and the rest is history," Ryan responded.

"If you say it like that, I guess so," I replied.

As if he had read my mind, Ryan said, "Don't worry about me asking a lot of questions. If it's something you want me to know, I'm sure you will tell me." He continued to put away the supplies at his desk.

That was okay with me and I'm sure if Ryan wanted me to know something, he would certainly tell me. Ryan didn't appear to be the shy type. Ryan was almost six-feet tall and seemed to be in excellent physical condition. He told me he had played football in high school and had planned on playing football in college but a knee injury changed all that. In fact, he said he didn't play football his senior year in high school.

The room was wide enough to have two of the same essentials on both sides of the room: a tall closet on either side of the door walking into the room, and two beds with only a mattress and two student desks. Each desk was furnished with a desk lamp and a chair. Sitting at the desk, the student would be facing the wall on their side of the room.

We only had a little over an hour before we had to meet in the Main Lobby for orientation so I started putting my things away and getting my side of the room ready for a two-week stay.

***

We all met in the Main Lobby at the designated time. Ryan and I had gotten to know each other a lot better in the past couple of hours. He would tell me about his time in high school and I told him about my high school career. He said he was elected to Vice President of his student class and was captain of the football team the year he played. Of course, I didn't have any stories like the ones he had but I did say something about almost joining the army.

The meeting at the Student Center lasted about three hours. We were given refreshments and sandwiches once we got to the conference room. Mr. Johnson introduced his staff to the group and we introduced ourselves by telling the group where we were from and what we expected to get from the program. Lucy, the receptionist from Assembly Hall, was on his staff, along with two other student workers and a State University guidance counselor. Mr. Johnson explained to us there were a total of 10 students in the two-week program.

Six males and four females from within a hundred-mile radius of the campus were invited to be in the program. The program was geared towards students that did not apply to a college but now might be thinking about going to college. The program would allow those students the opportunity to stay on a college campus and become a student for two weeks. Students in the program would also be allowed to check into and stay in a dorm, follow a three-class college schedule, and participate in any of the activities that the students attending full-time were participating in on campus.

Each roommate had the same class schedule. Although we were all taking math, history, and science, the classes were at different times of day. So, there were no more than two College Development students in one class.

Mr. Johnson also explained to us about the RA in the dormitory. The RA was short for Residence Assistant. That person was in charge of that particular floor in the dorm. The way it was explained to us was that the RA made sure hall parties didn't get out of control and that visitation hours were being followed. The RA would also unlock the door for us if we accidentally got locked out of our room. The residence assistant was a student that worked for the college but was also a student taking classes.

We received our class schedule. The location and class times were written on the pamphlet that Mr. Johnson handed out to us.

The orientation was very informative. We found out a lot about the campus and what to expect in the classes, as well as what to do if we had a nonlife threatening emergency or if we felt sick and needed to see the campus nurse. Mr. Johnson also told us that if we did well enough in the classes and decided we wanted to enroll at the university we would be given an exemption and allowed to enroll in the next semester. We would have to pay all of the expenses for the next semester.

Once the orientation was over, we were told we could go back to our dorm room or explore the campus if we liked. A couple of the students decided to walk around campus but Ryan suggested he and I should find out what building our first class would be in before we headed back to the dorm room.

———————————

After finding the building our first class would be in, we walked back to the dorm room. It was around 8:30pm when we finally made it back to the dorm room.

"What should we do now? All the orientation activities are over and we are free to do whatever we feel we should be doing...except, I don't know anyone here other than the students attending this program," Ryan said as he put his suitcase in his closet.

I was kind of surprised to see a somewhat sad look on Ryan's face turn immediately to a happy face with a huge grin. That meant he must have thought of something exciting to do for our first night on campus.

"Hey! Let's go down to the recreation room and play a few games of pool or watch some television. It's almost 9pm and the nights still early," Ryan said with some excitement in his voice.

"Okay, why not?" I responded. "I'm sure we can find something to do in the recreation room. I'm not too good at playing pool but I'm sure if I had a few practice games, I could do very well with that game."

Although the dorm was huge, it took about five minutes to walk down to the recreation room. A walk through the main lobby, down two flights of stairs, and past the laundry room led us into the recreation room.

The recreation room was a large open room that had a 32-inch television sitting on a huge TV stand located against the far wall of the room. Similar to the main lobby, there was a sofa and two chairs in a semicircle around the front of the television. Off to the right of the television and furniture, there was a large pool table with all the accessories--two students were already playing. But what really caught my attention was the ping pong table located across from the pool table. There were two females playing ping pong and a couple other females standing to the side watching the game. The only other person in the recreation room was a young man sitting on the couch watching television.

"Hi guys! Welcome to State University!" It was one of the females watching the ping pong match. Both Ryan and I looked at each other and said "Hi" at the same time.

"My name is Tanya, and my friend here is Lisa. She's my roommate. The two playing ping pong are Alicia and Missy. What brings you guys here?" Tanya was a slender, tall blonde who was attractive but not nearly as attractive as her friend Lisa. I knew Assembly Hall was a coed dorm but females were the last thing on my mind. Besides, I never expected Ryan and me to meet anyone at this time of night in the recreation room. Boy! Wasn't I wrong!

"We are part of the College Development Program and new to the campus," Ryan responded with some intelligence. I'm sure I had a dumb look on my face as I stared at the four females with my mouth frozen in the open position.

"We thought you guys might be freshmen. You guys have that new look about you. Relax. We are all students here. We just happen to be taking summer classes," Tanya said as she cheered on the female called Alicia.

"Where are my manners?" Ryan said loudly. "My name is Ryan

and my friend here with his mouth open is Star."

"Star? Now that's a very unusual name. How did you come by a name like that?" It was Lisa talking and saying my name! Why was it so difficult for me to talk at this moment? I don't recall ever having a problem talking to anyone, yet this interaction with these females caused me to lose all my ability for speech. Or was it just the one called Lisa causing me to have this trouble talking? No matter what it was, it was Ryan that came to my rescue again.

"Star said something about his uncle giving him that name. The same night he was born hundreds of stars filled the night time sky." Ryan waved his arms in an umbrella-like motion.

The ping pong match ended with Alicia and Tanya jumping up and down together saying, "We won! We won!"

After a few minutes of celebrating, they finally stop cheering.

"As you can see, we take these ping pong games very seriously. Each semester, the dorm holds a ping pong contest and the male and female winners along with their roommate are awarded a grand prize. There are only one set of winners per dorm and no student is allowed to win more than once during a calendar year. Since this is a coed dorm, we can have two winners: one male and one female. The prize for this semester are two tickets for a two-night stay at Disney World with paid transportation." Alicia had a smile on her face, but was still breathing a little fast from finishing the ping pong game.

"The idea is for one of our teams to win the tickets and we would all split the cost for two additional tickets. That way, the four of us would all have a chance to enjoy a short vacation to Disney World."

It was Tanya doing most of the talking for the four friends and Ryan doing all the talking for the two of us, but I did manage to ask a question. "When will the championship game be held?"

"So you can talk!" Lisa said, jokingly. "The championship game is held near the end of the semester before finals begin. That way, the game doesn't interfere with all the studying we will be doing to finish up the semester."

"Nice meeting you guys and good luck with that development course," Alicia said as she gathered her room keys and a small backpack. "Maybe you guys will like it here and decide to enroll. If so, we will see you around campus."

As they walked from the recreation room, Ryan's eyes lit up with excitement. "Star, I can't believe you were at a loss for words! No matter, I was always good at talking to females no matter their age. Stick with me and you won't have to ever worry about being tongue-tied again!" Ryan had the same excitement in his voice as he had in his eyes.

I didn't respond to Ryan comments but tried to change the subject altogether. "Ready for that pool game now? Looks like those guys are leaving."

Chapter 4
Two Weeks of Classes

I heard the alarm clock go off but was sure it was my imagination. Why would an alarm clock be going off in my room? My mom never said anything about placing an alarm clock in my room so I knew it must be my imagination. I really wanted to get back to the nice dream I was having about being named captain of the college basketball team. The team was cheering for me but I couldn't hear what they were saying because of the beeping from that alarm clock! Wait! That's a real alarm clock going off! I set it last night when Ryan and I returned from playing pool. If I recall correctly, it was around 3am! I have a math class to attend! I jumped from my bed in a panic but all I could see was darkness. Ryan was still asleep in his bed.

"Ryan! Wake up! We are going to be late for our first class! Ryan! Get up!" I said in a frantic voice. I never liked being late for class back in high school but I was on the verge of being late for my first class in college!

I finally saw a little movement from Ryan. I was looking for the clothes that I thought I had laid out to wear but remembered that I didn't lay out anything because I had spent half the night playing pool.

"Calm down, man!" Ryan said yawning and stretching his arms. "We have plenty of time to get ready and sit in that classroom. The class doesn't start until 8am. Did you check to see what time it is now?"

I was so worried that we were going to be late I forgot to check to see what the actual time it was.

"It's only 7:20 am so we have plenty of time to get to class. Of course, we will have to skip breakfast today because I don't think we will have time to have breakfast at the cafeteria and make it to class on time," Ryan said causally.

Ryan seemed to be older than his years. He didn't get too excited about anything. He'd been cool about everything we'd done since I met him for the first time the day before.

"Okay, Ryan. You're right. We do have time to make it to class on time, but I really don't want to miss breakfast!" I said as I tied my shoe.

"Not me. I hardly ever eat breakfast. So, if you want breakfast, you will have to get up a little earlier," Ryan said.

When we finished getting dressed, we gathered the supplies we needed for class. That was just the usual pen, pencil, and notebook. I'm not sure if I had the open mind to learn what Mrs. Wade spoke about, but I was sure that I would get it before the week was out.

We had learned most of what we needed in the Student Development Orientation the day before, so finding the class was not too difficult. All Ryan and I had to do was walk to the central-ized point on campus, which was the Student Center, and walk from there to Joseph C. Lynn Building. The JCL Building was where the math and science classes were held. It was a three-story building that had a large parking lot off to one side of the building. The parking lot wasn't open to the public. Students that had vehicles had to have a pass in their windshield and professors had to have an employee sticker in order to park there. The other parking lots around campus had similar rules for parking. The only place on campus that a sticker wasn't needed to park was in the dormitory parking lots. To park in those lots, a student identification pass was needed. All visitors were required to park in the visitor parking lot located next to the Student Center.

Since I didn't have a vehicle, the parking wasn't too important to me, but for Ryan, it was very important. Ryan drove a vehicle here for the two-week program but he was staying in the dormitory so he needed a student identification pass. At the orientation, Mr. Johnson said we were not allowed to keep a vehicle on campus since we were only staying for two weeks. But that wasn't communicated as clearly as they liked so a couple of students in the program drove their own cars. To keep those students from parking permanently in the visitor parking lot for two weeks, Mr. Johnson had to grant them an exception pass effective for two weeks just to park in the dorm parking lot.

Ryan and I were the only students from the development program in the introductory math class. The class began with the instructor giving us a syllabus on what to expect in the class in the coming weeks and how she expected everyone to show up on time for each and every class. The class was to last 50 minutes but the instructor cut the first class short by about 20 minutes because she said we would get started on Chapters one and two the next day. She also said that she expected everyone to read the first two chapters because there would be a "weekly knowledge test" at the end of the week. I'm not sure why she called it a knowledge test but having a test in the first week of school was new to me!

It turned out that the other two classes (astronomy and history) were similar to what was given in the math class the first day. The only exception was that instead of the end of week test, the test would be given on every other Monday morning for astronomy and once every three weeks for the history class. Ryan and I were scheduled for the same classes as the other roommates in the program. Mr. Johnson said it would allow the roommates to get to know each other and allow us to have someone to ask questions to if we ran into a problem. There was a good chance one of the two would have the answer to questions like where to find a certain building or what time a particular class was starting.

The first day of classes went without any major hiccups. Except for almost oversleeping, I think the day went very well. Unlike high school, there wasn't a teacher standing outside the room barking out orders to get into class and sit down or threatening a student that they would be sent to the principal's office if they didn't stop talking.

Between the history and astronomy class, Ryan and I decided to walk over to the cafeteria and have lunch. The lunchroom was a large open space with long six-foot tables and several round tables scattered throughout the cafeteria. Unlike back in high school, the tables here were not connected and we could sit anywhere we wanted to sit.

It just so happened that as we entered the cafeteria, Tanya and her roommate Lisa were leaving the cafeteria.

"Hi guys. Remember us? Too bad you guys didn't come for lunch sooner. Lisa and I could have used some company," Tanya said with a bright smile.

"Our class ended a little later than we expected. Maybe we can catch up with you ladies next time," Ryan responded cheerfully.

"Too bad you guys won't be around to see us win that ping pong contest," Lisa said, looking directly at me.

Once again, my mouth was frozen shut! How could this be possible? She was inviting me to talk but all I could get out of my mouth was….nothing!

Again, Ryan came to my rescue. "Star has had a tough morning. He didn't get a lot of sleep last night and was almost late for his first class." He patted me on the back.

"Yes, that happens sometimes. I think we all could use a little more sleep on certain nights," Lisa said as she looked at Tanya and then at me with what I thought was a smile on her face.

"Maybe we can watch you guys practice for your ping pong match later today or this week," Ryan said, as Tanya and Lisa walked away.

Tanya stopped, looked back, and said, "Maybe." Then continued to walk off.

⇒ ((◉)) ⇐

The two weeks of college went by like a snap of the fingers! It was the best two weeks that I'd ever had that included doing school work. Ryan and I became very good friends. He seemed to be older than his years in a lot of areas and I found myself looking up to him. We both did well enough in the classes to qualify for entrance in the next school semester and we met a lot of new people just by staying in the dorm and walking around campus. My sister didn't forget to come pick me up and my Mom was happy to see me when I returned home. My mom could tell that I'd had a great time at college because I wouldn't stop talking about it nor talking about certain females that I'd only met a couple of times during my two-week stay.

So, that was what college life would be like? I could come and go as I pleased and I stay up as late as I wanted! Why wouldn't I want to give college a try full-time? All I had to do was keep my grades up and stay out of trouble. Keeping my grades up might be a problem. I knew that Mr. Thomas said I could go to college and succeed but these college classes might be hard. I certainly wouldn't know if I could do college if I didn't commit to it on a full-time basis. I remembered what my Mother said also. I would have to find a way to pay for college myself. The only way I could get some quick money was to take out a loan from the bank, but I didn't have any credit and there was no way my mother, sister or brother would offer to help me get a loan. I could join the military for a couple of years and then come back and enter college, except that I would probably never come back to college. I had to find a way that would keep me around here. I remembered seeing something about the National Guard helping to pay for college. Why not join the National Guard? Maybe I could convince Ryan to join the National Guard with me. If Ryan joined with me, we could go together just to make the training a lot easier on the both of us. From what I'd heard about Basic Training, having a friend to go through that course was a good way to relieve a lot of the stress associated with becoming a soldier.

ROBERT L. WEAVER

Chapter 5
Joining the National Guard

Many young adults decide to join the military after high school or sometime during their early twenties. There are a few adults that decide to join the military when they turn thirty. The reason that young adults join the military varies upon the person. It could be because they want to serve their country and get a since of pride in serving, or it could be because their family is in need of money and the military is a quick way to earn money legally. Sometimes, like in my case, it was to earn money for college. No matter the reasons for joining and no matter the branch of the military, all men and women should know they are joining the greatest military force in the world. They must also know that by joining the military they are putting their lives at risk even in everyday training.

The cost of college without a scholarship can be extremely expensive. I was lucky enough to obtain a short-term loan to gain entrance into college my first semester. But I knew I had to find another way to earn money so what better way than to join the National Guard part-time. After all, once a month on weekends could not be that difficult! Not only that, the National Guard would pay for me to go to college! So, my plan was to join the National Guard with my friend, Ryan Callahan, whom I had met at the College Development Program at State College. In fact, the recruiter insisted that he could get both of us at the same training location and we could go through the basic training course at the same time. We would train at the same place to reduce the stress of being away from home and training with all new recruits.

My story of the military began on a Saturday morning after Ryan and I had returned from the recruiting station. It was near the end of our first semester at State University and we had returned to our dorm room to relax after a long morning at the recruiting station. We had filled out all the paperwork and the final step would take place on the following Monday when we were to sign all the legal documents and be sworn into the military. Ryan was lying on his bed with his legs stretched out and his hands clasped behind his head.

"Wow! What a long morning," he mumbled.

"Ryan, did you say something?" I was sitting at my desk going over the copies of the paperwork we had just filled out at the recruiting station.

"I don't know, Star. What does your mom think about you joining the National Guard?" Ryan asked in a quiet voice that made me look up from the papers I had been reading.

"She's all for it," I said happily. "I spent the last month of high school telling her and everyone else who would listen I was joining the military. I wanted to see the world at the military's expense. I know joining the National Guard is not the military and I won't get to see the world but it will help provide the money I need for tuition."

"My Dad is all for me joining something. I'm sure I can do it. The question is, do I really want to join the military?" Ryan asked as he continued to look up at the ceiling.

Ryan was as tall as me and weighed nearly 235 pounds. He was stocky but a good athlete. I'm sure he wouldn't have any problem with the physical part of joining the National Guard. As for myself, the physical part was really why I never put any real effort into joining the military.

"I talked to former students that joined the military and they told me horror stories about joining. Jim Bo Reed had joined the army last year. He's back home working at his Dad's garage. He said they didn't sleep much and the sergeants constantly stayed on him about something he wasn't doing correctly. He also said they made him walk for days and when he wasn't walking to go somewhere, he was running to go somewhere! I figured if I told everyone I was joining the army, they would think I was tough, but after hearing Jim Bo talk about his experiences, there was no way I was going to join the army! Now, I'm forced to join because I need the money."

"Just stop it, Star!" Ryan exclaimed loudly as he sat up to a sitting position on his bed. "You are not joining just because you need the money. You are joining because of that girl you met when we first arrived here at State University! Before you met her, you told me you were buying time until you could get a job and that you were not planning on coming back for this semester. Remember? You said you didn't think college was for you after that first week? When you found out she was enrolled here at the University, you started doing everything you could to ensure you were enrolled here also!"

Ryan paused to catch his breath. At the moment, I didn't have a response to his remarks. Then Ryan continued talking in a much quieter voice but now he was looking down at the floor of the dorm room.

"Me, I think I want to attend a college closer to my home and joining the military right now is not what I want to do. Joining will only keep me away from home longer than I want to be right now."

After hearing what Ryan had to say, there were lots of thoughts going through my mind. For one, how did he know I had feelings for Lisa? I never spoke about her to anyone. In fact, I'd only spoken to her a couple of times! And why should I tell anyone about a girl I've spoken to only a couple of times? It was none of anyone's business. And for two, Ryan was not going to join the military with me, so that meant I had to join alone. And three, more importantly, it was obvious that Ryan was having some issues back home that he didn't want to talk about with me.

"I don't know what girl you are talking about and why should I have a girl decide whether or not I attend college? I don't know what's going on back home with you but if you need to be there then I understand if you changed your mind about joining the Guard. You haven't signed any official documents so you are well within your rights to back out. If you need anything from me, just let me know." I said in the most understanding voice I could muster.

"Of all the guys I've met here at the University, you were

becoming one of my best friends, Star. I know I was a little hard on you about that girl you didn't think I knew about, but if that's who you like then I'm happy for you." That was all Ryan said and then he got up to leave.

"Where are you going?" I asked.

"I'm going down to the recreation room to watch television. Coming?" he responded.

"No, I think I'm going to hang out here for a while. I have some class work to catch up on and besides, I'm a little tired from the long morning we had," I said.

Ryan walked out and closed the door behind him as he left the room.

I received my orders a few weeks after signing the paper work that obligated me to join the Georgia National Guard. My orders were to spend 13 weeks of training at Ft. Benning, Georgia, beginning in June of the following year. I was to report to the bus station in town and from there, a recruiter would pick me up and take me to the training facility.

Until that time, I was to report each month to the local National Guard unit beginning in late January at 7am on Saturday and Sunday mornings. The National Guard unit was located in the city about seven miles from the college campus, so it was not a problem getting transportation to the unit because Ryan had planned to finish out the first year of college and since he had a car, he agreed to drop me off and pick me up on those weekends I was to report to the National Guard unit.

My first day at the unit found me being assigned to 1st platoon and Charlie squad by the one of the Sergeants. The unit was busy preparing for a training exercise that occurred every few years or so. After getting the proper uniform issued, I sat in the training classroom with the other squad members to listen to the briefing of the upcoming training exercise. I noticed that my uniform had my last name on one side of the front shirt pocket, and US Army on the other side of the front shirt pocket. I wondered why the National Guard uniform would have emblems from the US Army on it. At the time, I wasn't very concerned about what was on the uniform as long as the uniform fit!

Since I didn't have any formal training, there wasn't much for me to do except sit in the classroom with the other soldiers. During the training classes, I learned that the entire Georgia State National Guard Brigade would be headed to California in two months for a training exercise that would last for three weeks! The place was the National Training Center in California where war games would be carried out.

The recruiter never mentioned anything about going to California for three weeks! Now I was beginning to think there were other things about joining the National Guard that the recruiter failed to mention. Fortunately, since I had just enlisted and had not been to the basic training course, I was not required to go with the unit to the National Training Center!

What had I gotten myself into? I only joined the National Guard to make some extra money to help pay for college! I thought the National Guard helped out in the local community. As it turned out, the National Guards was more than a unit that helped out in the community. I learned in the classroom that this unit was just one of the units that made up a larger force. One unit was called a company. A company consisted of four to five platoons. Each platoon consisted of 30 to 35 soldiers each. So, in all, there were close to 120 soldiers in each company. There were eight to ten companies that made up the brigade. The entire training brigade would spend three weeks in a simulated war game against the opposing forces in the desert of California.

For the next few months, I attended the mandatory one-weekend-a-month training at the National Guard unit while I continued to go to school. During that time, I had little interaction with Lisa. Mainly, because every time I was around her, my tongue seemed to get tied. I had also failed to get Ryan to join the Guard with me so I was going to go through basic training alone. Each month at the Guard Unit, I was not required to do much more than sit in the classroom and occasionally listen to stories from different senior guardsmen adventures of training since I hadn't had any official training. The main topic was the preparation of the Guard Unit for the three weeks of training at the National Training Center in California. The NTC as it was called is where all the regular army units are cycled through for training about once every three years. It was simulated war games against what was called the Opposing Force or Op Force for short. The Op Force was made up of regular army units trained to fight like units from the opposing military. The main Op Force unit that was simulated was that of the Soviet Union. The Soviet Union had the only military in the world that could rival that of the United States. That was mainly because of the sheer number of tanks and planes that country owned. Although the Soviet Union outnumbered the U.S. in tanks and planes, those same tanks and planes were inferior to the tanks and planes of the United States.

Each month, I would sit in a class where one of the sergeants would talk about how the Soviet Union would deploy their troops and how the United States would counter what the Soviet Union deployed. Occasionally, those same sergeants would give a class on how the soldiers in the unit would handle a chemical attack by the Soviet Union. Just from listening to the training sergeant talk about a chemical attack or a nuclear bomb blast from the Soviet Union, I wished never to be a part of that. The chances of survival were extremely low in one of those attacks.

From what I could tell about the Op Force, it was a military that fought like the Soviet Union and did whatever the Soviet Union would do to destroy the military of the United States. Of course, all these training exercises were just training exercises, so all destroyed U.S. forces could come back and fight another day.

I continued to wonder if I had actually joined the Army, since each month at every class at the unit, a sergeant talked about military training and what to do in certain situations.

Meanwhile, I was doing okay with the college classes. I was keeping my grades up and staying out of trouble. Then one day Ryan told me he had mentioned to Lisa that I was joining the military. Of course, I couldn't hide the excitement in my eyes just to know what she said about that. But I tried. I immediately asked him why he'd had to tell her about me joining the Guard. He said he did it for my own good and because I would never have said anything to her if he didn't tell her. He also said I shouldn't be afraid to talk to her and it might be worth my while to get to know her. Ryan never told me what Lisa said to him. I would have to find that out by asking her myself.

Chapter 6
Basic Training

The time seemed to fly by and before I knew it, it was time to report for training. I had heard stories of the military being difficult on new recruits and today I would surely get a firsthand look at how difficult it could be for a new recruit. My orders came in the mail about three weeks ago. The orders were a 10 to 12-page document informing me of what day I would be placed on active military duty, when and where I was to report on that day, and how long my training would be when I was placed on active military duty. I'm not sure why there were four sets of these orders but that's what I received in the mail. I was also told in the orders to bring a copy of the orders when I reported to the base. I would go on active duty on the 27th, and would remain on active duty for 13 weeks. Those 13 weeks were broken down into six weeks of basic training and seven weeks of AIT (short for advanced individual training, I later found out).

Catching the bus to the city was a very simple task since the bus ride was about three hours long. The city bus station was where a sergeant from the base would meet me. We were told by the recruiter that all we had to do was wait at the bus station and someone from the base would meet us there. It turned out that I was not the only new recruit waiting for the sergeant. Once I arrived at the bus station and got settled in, I realized that other guys were waiting around also. At first, I thought they were waiting to catch the next bus out of town. But I heard a couple of them talking about military training so I concluded that they were waiting for the sergeant also.

When the sergeant arrived, he was easily recognizable since he was the only one driving a military van and wearing a camouflage green uniform crisply pressed with the sleeves folded up. He was also wearing black boots with a high shine to them with the pant legs from the uniform tucked neatly inside the top of the boots. He introduced himself as Sergeant Olivier.

"I'm Sergeant Olivier from Ft. Benning. Are you one of the recruits awaiting a ride to the base? If so, let me see your orders." The sergeant checked his list against my orders and followed the same process with the other recruits and then we proceeded to get in his van.

There were about seven of us, including the two guys that were talking about the military: me, and four other new recruits that had been waiting to be picked up by the sergeant at the bus station. We were all going to the Infantry Training Center for in-processing. I didn't know any of the first-time recruits as I sat down in the sergeant's olive green military minivan. Everyone was quiet except for one of the new recruits. This recruit had a big smile on his face. He was wearing a cowboy hat, jean shirt, and blue jean pants. He was the first to get on the bus but he didn't sit in the back. He sat on the first bench near the front of the bus. As each recruit entered the van, the guy that looked like a cowboy would greet him with a big "Howdy!" He spoke with a deep Texas accent. We all said hello and kept moving back to a seat. No one was talking except for him. It wasn't a surprise to us when he said he was from Houston, Texas, and that his name was Duke. I was surprised when he said this was his first trip away from home. Duke also said he had been on the bus since yesterday morning. After a while, Duke decided to stop talking because no one else was saying anything. I don't think we were trying to be rude by not talking. I think it was because we were going to the Infantry Training Center and wondering what the training would be like once we arrived. I think we all had heard stories of the training at the Infantry Training Center.

ROBERT L. WEAVER

The trip to the Training Center was not as long as I thought it would be. Maybe because Duke kept us entertained for a short while with his talking. As we drove through the city and onto the state highway, the scenery opened up, and there were trees on both sides of the road. After several miles we turned off the highway onto an off ramp. At the end of the off ramp there was an intersection. As we turned left onto the road, I noticed that the name of the highway as Infantry Way. Of course, there were more trees and a couple more intersecting roads along Infantry Way. The road led uphill and then back downhill and then up another steep hill. As we came down the second hill, we could see the training facilities.

The housing was two-story old wooden buildings. There were windows along both sides of the building, and wooden steps led up to a single doorway.

"Is that where we well be staying?" asked Duke.

"No.," said Sergeant Oliver. "That's Harmony Church. The new training facility is located on Sand Hill."

A big sigh of relief could be heard in that quiet van! We were all new to this military routine but none of us wanted to train in old World War Two facilities.

Once all the new recruits had arrived and assembled at the Sand Hill barracks, we were divided into four platoons consisting of about 30 to 34 recruits each. Each platoon was taken to a different floor in the building. The inside of the building reminded me of what the college dorm room at State University looked like. There was a main lobby area and doors leading to different wings of the building. Each wing had four floors and each floor could house one platoon. I was placed in First Platoon so we had a room located on the first floor of the building. There were no elevators in this building so a recruit that was in the fourth platoon had to walk up three flights of stairs to get to his room. There were two soldiers per room and I shared the same room with a recruit from Philadelphia named Hector. Since the day was almost over, the only thing we could do was assemble in the lobby after putting away our bags and have dinner in the mess hall. The mess hall also reminded me of the college cafeteria at State University. The only difference was that the tables were lined up in horizontal rows here at Sand Hill. The sergeant taking us to the mess hall had only one rule for recruits: no talking in the Mess Hall! Neither Hector nor I said anything while we ate our meal, but a couple of recruits could be heard talking here and there. The sergeant that was walking around the cafeteria only said, "Remember, no talking in the Mess Hall!" Those recruits that were talking continued to chat away. Once dinner was over, it was back to our rooms. Lights out was at 9pm sharp, and that's exactly when the lights went out!

Chapter 7
In-Processing

The next day found the entire company assembling for roll call at 6am. I always wondered how the military assembled in the morning and today I was getting a firsthand look at exactly how it was done. Roll call was where a platoon of soldiers assembled 10 to a row and four rows deep. One of the training sergeants would walk down the hall and knock on the door waking everyone up. There were four platoons assembling at the same time and each platoon had its own section. Each morning at in-processing, we were woken up and called to formation. I guess it was like a teacher making a roll call in a classroom to ensure all the students were present. After roll call, we all had a hot breakfast and then it was time to start the in-processing. The sergeants and lieutenants did not give us an itinerary as to what was going to happen. They just told us that the next three days would be for ensuring we qualified for military training. It consisted of giving the company (the combination of the four platoons) that all-important physical and uniforms called BDUs. I was beginning to learn that a lot of things in the military had abbreviations like the BDUs. That was short for battle dress uniform. It was a camouflage top and pant set that the U.S. Army issued to soldiers. I had to get used to those BDUs because it was the only type of clothing I was going to be wearing for the next 13 weeks.

Before we started to do anything, the first order of business was a visit to the barber. The entire unit was taken to a building that served as the barbershop. There were three chairs in this small building with three barbers waiting. So, three at a time, or when a chair was free, soldiers would enter this building to get a haircut. We were all from different backgrounds so we all had different hair styles. Some of those young men had very long hair and some had medium length hair. The barber would ask how you would like your haircut. The answer from many of the recruits would be "high and tight." This meant that a little hair would remain on the top of the head but nothing left on the sides and back of the head. It really did not matter the length of hair because those barbers only knew one way to cut. That was to cut the majority of the hair from the head! Having very little hair did not bother me. I was accustomed to having short hair.

After we had our hair trimmed, it was off to take a physical. Months ago, after I had signed the papers to join the National Guard, I did not think too much about the physical. I was given a physical back then and it only took about 45 minutes to an hour. At that time, I was more excited about getting the new uniform and the rest of the gear that would be issued to me than thinking about a physical. As it turned out, the physical at basic training was one of the most intense physicals that I had ever had! Those military doctors checked every soldier from head to toe and gave us shots that we'd never had before. Since there were so many soldiers getting a complete physical, the regular, single needle did not work. The military was very efficient in using a high-pressure needle gun. In less than 15 minutes, up to 30 soldiers could have all the required shots. The only instructions that were given were not to flinch. The doctors did not want to accidentally rip a soldier's shoulder with the high-pressure needle gun due the soldier moving as the shot was given. One of those shots had my shoulder sore for an entire day!

The physical that was given at in-processing was much more intense than the one that was given when I signed my name on the dotted line six or seven months earlier. I knew that there was a greater chance of something being found wrong with a physical such as the one the military was giving. Eyesight, chipped bones, old broken bones, and any other abnormality that could be found and checked out was tested by these doctors. A couple of recruits didn't pass the intense physical. My roommate told me that the physical revealed that he had high blood pressure and would have to be sent home. Although I was never diagnosed with high blood pressure, I tried to force myself to relax and not get nervous when it was my turn to have my blood pressure checked. My efforts paid off. The nurse told me I was fine.

In the military, one thing I had to get used to was hurrying up and then waiting. Since the physical was given in different areas of the training facility, we were rushed to each location. Some locations required the platoon to ride buses to get to them and others required that the platoon walk to the buildings. Regardless of where we had to go, it was always hurry up and get there! Once at the correct place, it was always about a half hour or more wait before any nurse came out to see any soldier.

In total, in-processing took about three days. The third day consisted of being fitted with the proper gear for training. It was almost like a human assembly line. Of course, after being rushed to get to the entrance of this huge building, we had to wait for an hour or longer to get processed through. Since my last name started with a letter near the end of the alphabet, I was near the end of the line and one of the last to go through. So, of course, my wait was a little longer than most other recruits.

Once I entered the building, I noticed a long winding counter with 20 to 25 different stations. Each station had a civilian worker busy asking questions and handing out equipment. The first station was where the soldiers were measured to receive shirts. A total of four shirts were given to each soldier. Somewhere behind that counter, a civilian worker sewed the last names of soldiers on their individual shirts. When I received my shirts, my last name had been sewn on them with the familiar U.S. Army flanking the last name. The next station was where we received our pants to match the tops.

The third station was where we received our hats. The next couple of stations consisted of being issued training gear such as a water canteen, utility belt, waterproof bag, ammo pouch, and a first aid kit. We didn't have time to actually try any of this equipment on because we were continually moving down the line. The transformation from civilian to soldier had begun now. The majority of the equipment was new. Things like the shirts, pants, and boots were new, but the water canteen and the utility belt weren't new out the box, but were very well maintained.

This seemed like a lot of supplies to carry around but the military made it very easy for us to transport all the new equipment we had just received. We were issued a green duffle bag to place all the equipment inside. Every recruit in the platoon had a duffle bag filled with all the equipment we were just issued. The only piece of equipment that wouldn't fit in the duffle bag was the rucksack. We were told that the rucksack was used to carry equipment when we trained in the field. Things like extra uniforms, socks, t-shirts and food could all be placed in that modified backpack called a rucksack.

Just like that, in-processing was over. On the final night, we were told to get a good night's sleep and be ready to get an early start because we were being sent over to the training facility where we would be housed so that we could complete the 13-week training.

Chapter 8
Physical Fitness

Physical fitness is probably the cornerstone of the military. Being able to walk or run for miles seems to be the goal given to every soldier, and every drill sergeant was bent on making sure every soldier was in top physical condition. The reality was that I was not in good physical condition. I thought back on the time I tried out for the football team in high school. I thought I had what it took to play a physical game but after one hour of tryouts, I soon realized I couldn't play football. When I joined the military, I had no idea what it would be like. No matter what, there were two reasons I couldn't quit. For one, I needed the money for college because I didn't have another way to obtain the money unless I joined the armed forces in a reserve role. The second reason was because it wasn't allowed! I could be put in a military prison or kicked out all together with a dishonorable discharge on my record or both! I only heard stories of what it was like to be a soldier. Now, I was a real soldier doing what real soldiers do on a daily basis. I remember seeing a slogan about the military once. That slogan read *'We Do More Before 9am Than Most People Do All Day.'* I never really understood what that meant until we started our first real day of training. I also learned that the intake grace period was officially over.

It was the loudest whistle that I had ever heard! I felt like I must have been dreaming because no one would be blowing a whistle that loudly at 4:30 in the morning! But before I had a chance to roll back over in my nice warm bed, the second loudest whistle I had ever heard rang in my ears. Only this time it was followed by, "SECOND PLATOON! FALL IN! OUT OF THOSE BUNKS! YOU HAVE FIVE MINUTES TO BE OUTSIDE STANDING IN FORMATION FOR PT!" It was the booming voice of Drill Sergeant Kelly.

I wasn't sure what "PT" was but I was sure I would find out soon enough.

"THE UNIFORM FOR PT WILL BE SHORT PANTS, ARMY T-SHIRT, AND RUNNING SHOES. YOU HAVE FOUR MINUTES TO BE OUTSIDE STANDING AT ATTTENTION IN FORMATION!" Drill Sergeant Kelly screamed. The only thing that registered in my mind was 'four minutes' and 'standing in formation.' I sprang out of bed and quickly put on the uniform that Drill Sergeant Kelly said we should be wearing for PT and ran as fast as I could to get in formation. As I ran downstairs and out the door of the barracks, I realized that it was still dark. I couldn't believe we were outside so early! The assembly area was located in front of the barracks and once I made it to the Second Platoon's area, I found my place and stood at attention, not daring to make a move. The only person I looked for was my assigned buddy. Fortunately, he was standing at attention next to me.

"ONE MINUTE!" It was Drill Sergeant Kelly's voice. He was inside the barracks but I could still hear his voice clearly! At that point, 99% of the entire training company was in formation standing at full attention. How could any soldier be late from that bone-rousing awakening?

"TIMES UP!" Drill Sergeant Kelly screamed. Somehow, he had made his way to the front of the company. First Platoon was positioned to my left in front of their assigned barracks. Second Platoon, the platoon that I was assigned to, was next in position. Third Platoon and Fourth Platoon were standing to my right in front of their respective barracks. Each platoon had a drill sergeant standing out in front. It was Drill Sergeant Cruz at the front of our platoon because Drill Sergeant Kelly had taken a position out in front everyone. It appeared he was the senior drill sergeant in charge of the entire company. I thought every soldier from each platoon had made his way out to the formation assembly area within the five-minute time frame but I was wrong because I could see a soldier running. It was a soldier from Third or Fourth Platoon that came speeding across the front of First Platoon and was just passing our platoon before he was called out. I'm not sure who that soldier was but his timing couldn't have been worse. To be late for the first official formation was not good. He came running out to the assembly area as Sergeant Kelly was screaming times up. It was the Third Platoon's drill sergeant that stopped the soldier in his tracks with a yell that would have stopped an elephant!

"STOP RIGHT THERE, TRAINEE!" said the drill sergeant. That soldier literally froze in his tracks. Every drill sergeant's attention was on that one soldier. It was kind of hard for me to see what was going on because I didn't want to move my head too much because any movement would draw the attention of a drill sergeant. But I was able to hear clear enough to know never to be late for a formation. "DROP AND GIVE ME TWO-FIVE," screamed the drill sergeant from Third Platoon to the petrified soldier. It was the first time that I had ever heard a drill sergeant order a soldier to drop and do push-ups (we were told at in-processing that 'drop and give me two-five' meant that we had to stop and do 25 push-ups on the spot). I had a strange feeling that it probably wouldn't be the last time that order would be given to a soldier during the next 13 weeks! That soldier immediately dropped down and started doing push-ups.

"IF ANYONE OF YOU ARE EVER LATE TO ONE OF MY FORMATIONS, THE PUNISHMENT WILL BE

PUSH-UPS. YOU WILL ALSO HAVE EXTRA DUTY AFTER WORK THE SAME DAY!" It was Drill Sergeant Kelly's booming voice. "THAT EXTRA DUTY WILL BE TO CLEAN THE OUTSIDE AREA OF THE BARRICKS FOR AN ENTIRE WEEK WHILE YOUR BUDDIES ARE RESTING AND RELAXING! I ASSURE YOU, YOU WILL NOT WANT ANY EXTRA DUTY AFTER WORK BECAUSE YOU WILL NEED ALL THE REST YOU CAN GET!" he continued.

"AS YOU ALL KNOW, WE ARE ONE TEAM HERE. WHEN ONE SOLDIER FALLS, WE ALL FALL! SO, ANYTIME ONE SOLDIER HAS TO DROP AND DO 25 PUSH-UPS, THE ENTIRE COMPANY WILL DROP AND DO 25 PUSH-UPS...COMPANY! DROP AND GIVE ME 2-5!"

That was totally unexpected. I get to formation on time and just because one soldier is late, we are all punished for his mistake? So, my start of training began with doing push-ups. The entire company of soldiers were counting off the number of push-ups completed... one, two, three, four and so on until we had completed 25 push-ups. I was struggling to get to 25 after the 14th one was completed. I was hoping the drill sergeants wouldn't notice me struggling to finish all the push-ups.

I was in luck. No one noticed me because Drill Sergeant's Kelly voice boomed out again.

"ON YOUR FEET! WE WILL MEET HERE EVERY MORNING EXCEPT SUNDAY MORNING FOR PT. IF YOU DON'T KNOW WHAT PT STANDS FOR, IT STANDS FOR PHYSICAL TRAINING. WE WILL BE DOING EXACTLY WHAT IT STANDS FOR EVERY DAY SIX DAYS A WEEK. IF IT RAINS, WE WILL BE DOING PT. IF IT SNOWS, WE WILL BE DOING PT. GOT IT?"

"Yes, drill sergeant!" The entire company responded just as we were told how to respond during in-processing but it wasn't loud enough because Drill Sergeant Kelly said, "I CAN'T HEAR YOU!" In unison, the entire company repeated 'yes, Drill Sergeant' as loud as we could.

It took about five minutes to march over to the huge parade ground where PT was held and for the next half hour to forty-five minutes, we all followed one of the drill sergeant's lead doing stretching and jumping jacks. I can't be sure of the time because no trainee had a watch. Only the drill sergeants were allowed to keep watches and what private in their right mind would ask any of the drill sergeants the time of day!

We had to have a partner to help us do sit-ups so the soldier directly behind us was to be our partner. In order for the sit-up to be correct, the trainee doing the sit-up would clasp both hands behind his head while sitting on the ground with both knees bent and both feet together. Using mostly stomach muscle, the trainee would sit completely up with both hands still clasped behind his head until his head was at a position between his knees. Only then was the trainee allowed to go back to the starting position. My job as the partner was to ensure the trainee did not move while doing sit-ups. I would place a hand on each ankle and hold them in place on the ground. By holding the trainee's ankle and not allowing the trainee to have any significant movement in any direction, the trainee could complete the sit-up correctly. Once a partner was finished with his set of sit-ups, the positions would be switched and the trainee holding the feet would get a chance to do his set of sit-ups.

After the all sit-ups were completed, we then started with push-ups. There were a couple of things I found out about doing push-ups in the army. One was to keep both hands flat on the ground. The second was to keep your back and legs straight at all times while bending at the elbows to go down and then come back up. Sounds simple enough. But not in the army! In the military, push-ups and sit-ups had to be performed in the correct way or they wouldn't count. I could hear the Drill Sergeants walking around correcting soldiers on how to do whatever exercise we were doing at the time. The majority of the trainees completed the sit-ups correctly because I didn't hear the drill sergeants correcting many trainees on how to complete that drill. Occasionally I would hear a drill sergeant say, "ALL THE WAY UP, TRAINEE!" or "KEEP THOSE HANDS BEHIND

YOUR HEAD!" The yelling could be heard coming from various places across the assembly area.

It seemed like the drill sergeants paid extra attention to trainees doing push-ups to make sure the push-up was being completed correctly.

I knew I wasn't the only soldier struggling to keep up on the first day of PT. I could hear the moans from other soldiers as we went through each drill. It became apparent that I was way out of shape and that this was going to be a very difficult thirteen-week campaign.

"YOU CALL THAT A PUSH-UP? MY GRANDMOTHER CAN DO BETTER THAN THAT! DO IT AGAIN TRAINEE BUT THIS TIME, KEEP YOUR BACK STRAIGHT!" that was Drill Sergeant Kelly correcting a soldier on how to do a push-up except it sounded much louder than ever before.

"ARE YOU LISTENING TRAINEE, OR DID YOU COME TO PT WITH EARPLUGS IN YOUR EARS?" the Drill Sergeant continued.

That's when I realized I had my eyes closed. I opened my eyes and looked up and Sergeant Kelly was standing in front of me staring down at me with a bone-chilling stare on his face! It took all I could do to respond in the proper manner.

"Yes, Drill Sergeant." I could barely get that out!

"I CAN'T HEAR YOU!" said Drill Sergeant Kelly in a voice that seemed to make the earth move!

"YES, DRILL SERGEANT!" I yelled at the top of my lungs hoping it was loud enough.

I never knew I could yell as loud as I yelled that response! Drill Sergeant Kelly didn't say anything else to me. He moved on to another soldier to correct how that soldier was doing his push-ups.

I was trying not to draw attention to myself but I was in terrible physical shape, so that seemed like an impossible task. I wasn't sure how to avoid standing out except by getting into better shape.

Finally, the exercise drills came to an end. We were all standing in formation so I had a chance to catch my breath. It was still dark out with the only light coming from the lights on tall poles located at intervals around the assembly area. We could now go back to the barracks and get some much-needed rest! My throat was dry and I was feeling about as terrible as I could feel. It had been about an hour to the best of my knowledge, and I couldn't wait to get back to the barracks to sit down!

"ATTENTION!" bellowed Drill Sergeant Kelly. We all stood at attention waiting to be dismissed to go back to the barracks.

"IT'S TIME FOR OUR DAILY RUN"! A SOLDIER WHO DOES NOT COMPLETE A DAILY RUN WILL HAVE EXTRA DUTY!" the Drill Sergeant continued.

I was completely caught off guard from hearing about a daily run. How was I going to complete a daily run when I could barely get through the push-ups?

The road that led to the barracks was a little more than three miles from the state highway. The road was called Knock Out Lane by the trainees, but its real name was Infantry Way. Infantry Way led directly to the training facilities so anyone that had business on the training facilities had to take this road. Knock Out Lane was the road we took for the Company's daily run. It was a paved road that had a hill on it about every mile. Riding in a vehicle, the hills were not as noticeable. Walking or running on this road was a completely different story.

After completing the required stretching, sit-ups, and push-ups, each platoon would line in column of fours. Everywhere the entire company traveled, the order was always the same. We would always travel in column of fours with First Platoon leading off and then Second Platoon, Third Platoon, and Fourth Platoon. It was no different when we had our daily run. I imagine it was an awesome sight to see that large column of soldiers standing tall and running down the highway in perfect unison! Of course, we were nowhere near being in perfect unison on the first day!

The march to the road was about a quarter mile and it seemed like we were walking to a place of doom. If any of the other trainees were tired and out of breath at this stage, they were hiding it extremely well, because unlike earlier, it was not as noticeable. I couldn't hear a lot of heavy breathing (except from me!) and it was darker as we moved away from the physical training area so I couldn't see the faces of any of the other trainees.

A company or platoon on the move required a couple of things. One was the flag bearer and the other was a couple of road guards. Each platoon supplied its own flag bearer and road guards. The soldier that carried the flag for the platoon was always in front of the column but behind the drill sergeant leading the column. The road guards would run along beside and in front of the column to stop any approaching traffic and to stop vehicles at intersections. Both of these positions were manned by trainees who volunteered from the platoon. Usually, the volunteers were the same trainees each day. If a volunteer trainee was knocked out during the run due to some misfortune, another volunteer trainee would take that trainees' place. Only the road guards were allowed to wear the bright orange vest with a night light so they could be seen clearly in the dark. As the column approached traffic, one of the four road guards for the platoon would run to where the traffic was approaching and stop the traffic until the platoon passed by. As the next platoon approached, the road guard from the next platoon would run up to take the place of the road guard in the platoon ahead of them. Being a road guard required being in shape. Although that trainee had to a chance to rest while the platoon passed, that same road guard had to run a little harder and faster to catch back up with his platoon and take his position on whatever side he had in the column on that day. Needless to say, I was far from ready to volunteer to be a road guard or a flag bearer!

As we started to run (at a slow pace to start out), I was thinking that it might not be as terrible as I had imagined. My legs and arms were still hurting from doing all the exercises along with the push-ups and sit-ups, but the running seem to be relaxing my muscles. At this slow pace, I felt I could run for days! At that point the drill sergeant had started to sing as we ran. The singing kept the column in step so we wouldn't look like mob running down the road. It also helped to build running endurance.

Once the drill sergeant started to sing the song about Jody and his girl, the wall came crashing down on me! That good feeling I had was during the first half mile. Not because Jody girl left him while he was away in the Army as the song indicated, but because by the time we had reached the end of the first mile, the speed of the column had picked up and we were running at a much faster pace (I thought we were running at a pace too fast for the first day!). The singing on top of the running was too much for me! I could barely keep my breath, much less sing a song while running! Up the hill we went and now I was really feeling terrible. My legs hurt, my head hurt, and it felt like my chest was about to explode.

It turned out that a few trainees were in worse shape than me because I could hear the drill sergeant saying, "GET BACK INTO FORMATION, TRAINEE! THIS RUN ISN'T OVER!"

About a mile from the barracks, I could see that road guards from First Platoon were coming back towards the training column. We were turning around and heading back to the barracks! At this point, we were at the top of the first hill on Infantry Way. As we headed back downhill towards the barracks, the yelling from the drill sergeant continued. "GET UP TRAINEE!" Another trainee was struggling to continue the run. In fact, there were two trainees sitting on the side of the road.

About halfway down the hill headed towards the barracks, the column turned around again! We were now headed back up the hill. This was almost more than I could bear. The drill sergeant continued to sing his songs and for the most part, the majority of the Company sang with him. Except me. My singing had stopped about a mile back. Right now, I was just trying to breathe and force my legs to take steps! I kept telling myself it would be over soon. We made the turn back downhill headed towards the barracks and this time we didn't stop (or slow the pace) until we were at the assembly area.

Finally, it was over. I was exhausted! It seemed like every part of my body hurt. But I could say that I made it through the first PT of training! We now stood not at attention but in an "at ease" state awaiting the drill sergeant's instructions.

"TRAINEES!" It was Drill Sergeant Kelly speaking from the same spot he occupied before we started running.

"TODAY WAS THE FIRST RUN OF MANY RUNS IN THE NEXT THIRTHEEN WEEKS. SOME OF YOU DID VERY WELL, SOME OF YOU STRUGGLED, AND A COUPLE OF YOU DIDN'T COMPLETE THE RUN. TODAY WILL BE THE FIRST AND LAST DAY ANY TRAINEE FAILS TO COMPLETE A RUN! WE ARE ONE TEAM HERE AND PART OF BEING A TEAM IS MAKING SURE ALL TEAM MEMEBERS FINISH WHATEVER WE ARE DOING. IF YOU HAVE TO PUSH, PULL, OR DRAG YOUR TEAMMATE, YOUR TEAMMATE WILL FINISH! ANY MEMEBER OF A PLATOON THAT DOESN'T FINISH A RUN, THE ENTIRE PLATOON WILL BE ON EXTRA DUTY! YOU HAVE FIFTEEN MINUTES TO BE STANDING IN FRONT OF THE MESS HALL WITH FIRST PLATOON BEING FIRST. DISMISS!"

Chapter 9
M16A2 Weapons Qualification

Okay, thinking back to my time growing up as a kid, I never liked guns. I always thought guns were loud and it seemed each time that I had ever heard anyone talk about a gun, it was how someone had used a gun to shoot someone else. On a few other occasions, I heard people talk about using a gun to hunt deer for food but I could never bring myself to shoot a poor helpless deer. I do understand that hunting is a hobby for some people and just because I don't personally care for the sport doesn't mean I should tell other people how they should think about it. Way back when I first decided to join the military as a young teen, it was mainly because of the commercials on television. On those commercials, not once did they mention anything about having to actually use a weapon. What I really got from those commercials was the fact that I could wear a cool-looking uniform and travel the world. I never gave much thought as to what I would actually be doing once I joined the military.

This week I would have my first taste at qualifying for a weapon. That weapon is the M16A2 rifle. Note to self: do not call that weapon a gun! Drill sergeants really get bent out of shape when a recruit makes the mistake of calling that rifle a gun. Push-ups, extra duty, or any other job that required a recruit to do something extra would be in that poor recruit's future. From what the drill sergeants tell us, it's the best rifle in the world and we should treat it as such.

Long before we ever got a chance to fire our first shot, we had to learn how to disassemble the M16 in two minutes. And to really challenge us, we also had to reassemble it in another two minutes. I thought I would never learn that process but after disassembling it to clean it daily (and sometimes twice a day) it became second nature. It was the weapon of choice for the U.S. military. It might be used one day to help keep a soldier alive, so it needed to stay in good working condition. We had to do our part in keeping it free of dirt and dust. Everywhere we went to train, that weapon was with us. The drill sergeants never said anything about why we had to keep it with us at all times but I think it had something to do with the new recruits getting accustomed to always having it with them.

At the end of each day, we would spend 45 minutes to an hour taking the rifle apart and cleaning it. A drill sergeant would inspect it to insure we had it cleaned to "army regulation." That meant there couldn't be a speck of dust in the firing chamber nor inside the barrel of the weapon.

To qualify for the M16A2 rifle, a recruit must first zero the rife. The rifle would be unique to each individual soldier's firing style. The site mechanism of the weapon in terms of windage and elevation was unique to each individual soldier. Yes, it was possible that another soldier could fire a different soldier's weapon but the accuracy of the soldier with another soldier's weapon would probably be off by a great deal.

Although I grew up in the country, I never fired a hand gun or a shotgun. But to my surprise, learning how to fire the M16 rifle was not as difficult as I thought it would be. But I was only one recruit out of a platoon of 30. A couple of the recruits had a somewhat more difficult time.

In order to zero and qualify, we had to practice with live ammunition and each day we would travel to the rifle range to practice. The rifle range was broken up into two ranges: a smaller range where a soldier would zero his weapon, and a larger range where a soldier would practice shooting at pop-up targets. On the smaller zero range, there could be as many as 10 recruits firing at one time and the larger range could have up to 20 recruits at one time. Each range required every recruit to pay detailed attention to his surroundings, and this point was stressed by the drill sergeants each time we were on either of the ranges. Two of the most important rules while on the firing ranges were, one, the assumption that every weapon was loaded with a live round, and, two, that a soldier should always keep the barrel of the rifle pointed downrange away from the troops. Sounds simple enough, but by now I was a lot smarter in my estimation then some recruits. My thinking for the rest of training was that I should always pay attention to my surroundings and never ever let anyone walk behind me while on the rifle range or any other live ammunition range!

In my experience so far in training, there was always a recruit that would do something he shouldn't do. Ninety-nine percent of the time, it was a mistake on the recruit's part, either by not following directions or just not paying attention. In my platoon, it was the recruit called Southerland.

Since Southerland begins with an "S" and my last name began with a "W", we were kind of close in a lot of training exercises. Not close as in friends but close simply because the first letter in our last names were close together. The military seemed to do everything in alphabetical order! It didn't take me long to realize Southerland was one of those recruits that, if something was going to go wrong, he would be in the middle of it! Fortunately, Southerland was in front of me on many of the training exercises so I never had to worry about something happening behind me. But I could plainly see trouble brewing right in front of me when it came to Southerland and the rifle range. Most people can distinguish the right from the left but when something was added (in this case a rifle with the barrel that had to always remain pointed downrange) sometimes it takes a split second to figure out what side was the right and what side was the left. Southerland knew his right from his left but he forgot all about the rifle barrel having to always be pointed downrange.

We had to fire from a foxhole that was made completely of concrete. The foxhole was about five feet deep with room enough for two soldiers. There were 10 foxholes on this range. They were spaced about fifteen feet apart and each soldier had to drop down into the foxhole since there were no steps leading down into it. Two twenty-round magazine clips were given to each recruit before we headed out to the foxhole. We had to keep the clips inside the ammo pouch on our utility belt until we were told to remove them. We also had to keep both hands on our rifle until we reached the foxhole where we would set the rifle down on the ledge of the foxhole and wait until the drill sergeant told us to enter the foxhole all at the same time. Basically, we didn't come into contact with the live ammunition until we were safely in the foxhole facing down the firing range.

Everything seemed to be going according to plan. We had been divided up into groups of 20 and with two soldiers to a foxhole. Southerland was in front of me but he was not my foxhole partner. The Drill Sergeants had issued us our live ammunition to use for practice and as a group we were ordered to head toward the foxholes in a single file ten feet apart. Remember, the rifle barrel must always stay downrange away from any of the other soldiers or drill sergeants. The first set of soldiers would occupy the first foxhole, the second set of soldiers the second foxhole and so on.

Halfway down to my assigned foxhole, Southerland decided to turn around! I have no idea why he chose to turn around at that particular time and head back towards the entrance. Needless to say, I was shocked to see him heading back towards me with his rifle pointing away from the range! I stopped and I hoped the two recruits behind me had stopped also. As soon as I stopped walking, all I could hear was the drill sergeant shouting at Southerland to stop walking and to lay his weapon down on the ground. To my surprise, Southerland actually stopped! I don't know if it was just a moment of Southerland forgetting where he was at and hearing the drill sergeant (who just sped by me like a streak of lightning) shouting his name caused him to stop or he just stopped on his own accord. Whatever the case, Southerland was in for a lot of extra duty this week! Fortunately, no one was hurt and the remaining of the weapons qualification went as planned by the drill sergeant.

I'm not sure how I did it but I managed to qualify as an expert shot! It turned out that learning how to shoot a rifle wasn't as difficult as I thought it would be. Just listening and following what the drill sergeant asked us to do was what I attribute it to.

Chapter 10

Return to Home and School

B asic training was finally over. I was finally back at home waiting for the next semester in school to start so that I could continue my college career. My mom was very happy that I actually followed through on something I said I was going to do. She said I looked different and talked differently now that I was back from basic training. It was not uncommon for the military to change a person. I was a lot more disciplined in the things that I did now. There were a couple of reason I joined the Guard, but the most important reason I joined was to acquire the money to stay in college. That College Development Program actually changed my life. If I had not attended the two weeks at State University, I would never have known what college life was like. Not to mention I would not have met a certain female who was enrolled there full-time.

I'm sure my roommate would disagree with me on the reasons I joined. He probably would say, "Star, just stop it! You only joined the National Guard to impress Lisa. The only way you could get the courage just to speak to her was to join something as dangerous as the military!"

I learned a great deal about myself during basic training. Before joining, I didn't think I could meet the challenge physically or mentally of becoming a soldier. I lacked the physical strength and mental toughness it required on a day-to-day basis. I was out of shape and seemed to look for excuses not to do things that were required of me.

During the first couple of months after joining the Guard, I was not a qualified infantry soldier. The only way to get qualified was to attend that thirteen-week class and train alongside soldiers who were training to become full-time army soldiers and other recruits who were training to become soldiers in the army reserve.

Basic training allowed me to gain the mental toughness that I lacked. It taught me how to look at problems and meet them head on. For me, it was a tremendous learning experience.

I now realize that the term "weekend warrior" meant more than just putting in a two-day weekend and the obligations of attending a "weekend drill." National Guardsmen are soldiers. They qualify and train with the same equipment as the regular army and army reserve soldiers. One day, a National Guardsman may have to put his or her life on the line to defend this great country.

By being put in difficult situations during training, I've learned to adapt to my surroundings and take on problems head on. Before basic training, I didn't feel I could take responsibility for my actions nor take criticism. Now, I know I can be a man, take responsibility for my actions, and grow from constructive criticism. Not all criticism is meant to be bad. Learning to understand what's being criticized and making a point to learn and grow from mistakes was a big key to completing basic training.

In a few weeks, I could walk proudly across the campus of State University because I knew I could accomplish anything I set my mind to accomplish. The countdown to my return to college had begun. Now it was only a matter of weeks before the semester started. Relaxing at home was different from relaxing at home after graduating from high school. I actually got a chance to relax this time. My Mom didn't ask me to go out and look for a job. In fact, a couple of store owners in town called my house to offer me a job just until I returned back to college!

The first stage of my military career was finally over. I held the rank of Private First Class (or PFC for short) in the National Guard. That rank held the same responsibilities as a full-time Army soldier with the same rank. In the upcoming months in the National Guard, I would learn that PFC was a very unique position in the military. I would eventually have to make a decision whether to move onto the second stage of my military career or just continue to keep the rank of Private First Class! But that's a topic for another time. Right now, I just want to focus on enrolling back into college and living the college life with a sprinkle of the military life on the side!

The End